T0065491

Adriana Dardan

authorHOUSE®

AuthorHouse™
1663 Liberty Drive
Bloomington, IN 47403
www.authorhouse.com
Phone: 833-262-8899

Published by AuthorHouse 03/16/2021

ISBN: 978-1-6655-1984-7 (sc)
ISBN: 978-1-6655-1983-0 (e)

Print information available on the last page.

This book is printed on acid-free paper.

Dedicated

To those who aim at the stars with aspirations and hopes raised by their moral values, which are held and cherished in the noble core of the human being.

Adriana Dardan

Contents

Foreword

Everyone has a story to tell, whether it is real, fictional, or inspired by reality and enriched with imaginary details. First of all, the narrator or writer considers the probability of acceptance of the narrative by a benevolent audience that is interested in description of the subject and of the characters that evolve along the way. Most of the time, the subject is paramount in the narrative and the characters are gradually formed in accordance with the need to emphasize the concrete facts. Often, however, the narrator chooses priority over characters at the expense of the subject, emphasizing the development of each personality as events become a need to more accurately outline the motivation of behavior, thinking, and feelings of each participant in the story. With the evolution of the characters a new segment of action appears as a necessity in the continuation of the subject that develops gradually. As the characters progress in complexity, the subject of the narrative becomes the motivation that explains the course of action.

If this accomplishment is met successfully, the narrative is accepted by the reader and represents the great reward for the one who developed it.

Adriana Dardan

Chapter 1

Breezy Wind

Summer days in southern Texas are mostly sunny, with blue sky, and a few fluffy clouds moving slowly like in a gracious dance after a music heard only by them. The fields below, stretched to the limits of view show the rich wheat crop, grown about four feet tall, caressed by a gentle breeze, which makes them look alive.

The most extensive agricultural land is in the Mc.Mullen county, with a very small population, and which is considered the wealthiest in the state. It's county seat is Tilden, where luxury homes are not in shortage and which usually reach prices that only wealthy people can afford. Austin, the capital city of Texas, is not far from Tilden, and is the location of the best university in the state.

About ten miles far from Tilden, there was a farm around four hundred acres, which was the property of a couple, Nora and Philip Doukas.

From the highway, on the right side, it could be seen an iron forged portal on top of which was written the word *LANTANA*. A country road about less than one mile length led the way to the front side of a two-story colonial mansion, situated on the East site, extremely elegant, and which displayed wealth and prosperity. On the far site, it was the silo where grain was stored; next to it was a shed where equipment, machinery, and power tools were kept; the fuel storage tank was located below ground, far from the nearest structure. On the other side, across the shed, was a building where field farm workers were provided with housing accommodation, and next to it, a small building was the home of the manager, Joshua Reid and his wife Mya. About four to five hundred yards far from their building, on the right side of the farm, one could see a majestic oak tree, like watching the fields.

The mansion had five bedrooms, four bathrooms, a huge living room, study, and four other rooms with different purpose, which actually nobody cared to use. The furniture was exquisite and highly expensive, priced at the level of only big money can buy. A standard size piano, in the main hall, was Nora's delight, who liked music and played from time to time. The kitchen was designed with the most modern appliances to ease the preparation of food and to make a pleasant surrounding for those in charge. The personnel responsible for the smooth running of the household were Betty the cook and Irene the housekeeper who were housed in a homey building next to the garage.

The mansion had an additional small structure on the side, which was the laboratory where Philip Doukas, professor at Austin University, worked on his scientific research projects in Biotechnology. From the area of the farm, about ten acres were reserved for the experimental studies, conducted to validate the hypothesis of his research on photosynthetic organisms at molecular level. The first stage of Philip's experiments were performed in a glass greenhouse, which was right next to the laboratory building and where his assistant was supervising the procedures established for the development of new plant specimens.

Philip was the third generation of Greek immigrants and the first in his family to reach a high education and an easier way to make a living. His grand-grand parents were poor and worked as seasonal laborers wherever they could find a job. Farming was the place most sought by those who could do hard work, accept low pay, and were content to make a living from one day to the next. In spite of the hard life, they learned about farming in all details and transmitted to the next generation everything they knew and what could help in making a living with fewer struggles. Even if Philip's father never could buy a farm, and only worked as a laborer, he learned from him the thin and thick about growing crop in all weather conditions and about everything a skilled farmer should know. He worked next to his father since he was barely a child, and by growing up, he decided to learn more and get an education, which could help him to become the first in his family to have an intellectual life. He went to school, working in the same time on the farm, and his ambition to succeed led his determination to go all the way up to graduate from the university with the highest academic degree. He decided to study the structure of plants at the molecular level, conduct research projects on photosynthetic organisms, and find the best ways to grow new species with more health benefit. After acquiring his doctorate degree, Philip became professor at the university, and in the same time, he pursued his strong desire in developing research projects, by working long hours in the laboratory. He would have liked to own his place of study and a small farm to test the reliability of his hypothesis by experimenting the new findings developed under the microscope. Nevertheless, he was at the beginning of his career, coming from a poor family, not having any support besides his salary, and having a farm and a place of study was just a dream which could not be fulfilled, at least for the time being.

On his way up to a successful career, Philip wrote and published several papers, and became one of the youngest scientists in his generation to be recognized as having great potential to develop new advancements in the molecular research on photosynthetic organisms, and in expanding complicated experiments for new forms of plant species. From time to time, Philip was invited by reputable institutes and organizations to give lectures with subjects in his field of research.

In that day, he prepared a speech about the impact of climate changes on vegetation, especially on plants in the fragile stage of germination. The auditorium was packed with people mostly interested in the subject, joined by others who came just out of curiosity to learn about a topic which was a controversial issue in the ecological environment.

Philip started his speech, as usually, addressing the audience in the most professional way, in a very assertive mode, conquering the attention of the listeners in a complete quiet atmosphere. In the front row seat, a very elegant and attractive woman watched carefully his self-confidence, his baritone voice, the look in his eyes, and his occasional smile. He was very handsome, with light brown hair, gray blue eyes, fair complexion, a body well built, and an aristocratic posture. Philip became the subject of that woman's total attention, in the very small details, carefully observed, and recorded in every aspect. She didn't hear a word of his speech, since she was not interested a bit in that scientific topic, which was very far from her curiosity.

Nora Wilson was born in the city Midland nicknamed *The Tall City* located in the Permian Basin, the largest petroleum producing area in West Texas. Her parents owned quite a big number of oil wells, which made them multi-millionaires in the highest rank of wealthiest people in the county. They lived in a mansion where everything inside was at the level of the outward showing the most luxurious elegance. Nora grew up in a boarding school for rich and even richer girls, not cultivating special feelings for her parents and her brother. She went to college and graduated in Business Administration, considering that she had to know everything about managing the wealth waiting for her. When her parents died in an airplane crash, she inherited half of the fortune left her to be managed wisely and profitably to be increased. Her brother who knew well the price of money and had big plans to increase his part of the wealth, inherited the other half.

Nora traveled a lot, everywhere she could find excitement, rich people to share pleasures, and places which could captivate her imagination and her feelings. Quite often she traveled to Austin, where she bought a luxurious apartment with the view of the city and where she met with friends of her league. She was married to an aviator who proved to be unfaithful, and not that she cared about, but for many reasons the marriage didn't work out. Here and there, she found a male companion, always ready to go wherever she wanted, and be at her disposition with everything she asked. Nora was a woman who could spend money without giving an account to anyone; she could fulfill all her desires, all her pleasures, and all her needs, without having anyone to ask about her expenses. Apparently, she couldn't be more satisfied in her life. Nevertheless, people are never content with what they have, and there is always something missing to make them happy. In Nora's life the only piece of her jigsaw puzzle, which she badly wanted, was fame and glory. She needed a name with high recognition in the world of the most intelligent and sophisticated minds. In that evening, while staring at Philip, she knew that he was the man with the name she eagerly desired, and she will have him at any price, no matter the cost. She didn't think for a moment that he might be married, or engaged, or have the love of his life next to him, or have a family with problems. Her decision to have him was enough powerful to give her strength to make her eliminate everything and everyone who would be in her way.

A round of huge applauses woke her up from the dream of the decisions she just made. Philip finished his lecture and people were invited in the main hall for a glass of champagne. Nora sent home her companion and joined the others who gathered for commentaries or a casual talk. Colleagues and strangers who congratulated him, exchanging a few words with each other, surrounded Philip. Nora waited for her moment when she could see him alone, thinking in the same time that she has to be very cautious when talking with him, measuring each word coming out of her mouth, and avoiding in this way any embarrassing situation. She was not in his league of the highly intelligent and knowledgeable minds, but she was not naïve either. After a while, people started to leave the hall, and Nora was close to the door when Philip was about to get out.

"Congratulations, Doctor Doukas, your lecture was extremely compelling. It was a real pleasure for me to attend it. I am Nora Wilson."

"Thank you Ms. Wilson for your kindness. Are you interested in my field of research?"

"I am, but only as an amateur. The environment is a general problem, which is on the platform of discussion at any level of knowledge, since people of every socio economic status are concerned about."
"I'm glad you said that. What is your field of working?"

"Business administration with specific branch in oil and gas industry. Probably, the oil and gas pollution is one of the worst around, and one of your biggest concerns."

"Pollution is not my expertise, but is adjacent to the difficulties to keep a clean climate for the vegetation in my projects of research. It was a pleasure talking to you, Ms. Wilson, and I hope we'll meet again. I must go now, I am very tired, and tomorrow I have to lecture in front of my students who are less amiable than my listeners in the auditorium are. Good night."

"Good night, Doctor Doukas."

Philip went home to his modest apartment, which looked more like a bookstore with hundreds of books on shelves and around, combined with an office where everything on his desk was a mess. He took a shower and went to bed, forgetting all about that nice woman who talked to him in a very distinguished style.

Nora decided to give him some time without being in his way. She flew to Midland, her home town, to check the accounting books and see how much money was added to her inheritance. The numbers were very satisfying and promising. After a few days she was ready to go back to Austin.

"You're not staying longer?", her brother asked.

"No. I have many things to do, and cannot stay."

"Who is this time? Someone I know?"

"No. I have to leave now. I'll see you in a couple of weeks, or so. Bye, Jack."

Next morning, Nora went to the university and watched the door of the building where she knew Philip was working, waiting for him to show up. Around lunchtime, he came out, carrying with him the briefcase that was always filled with papers and never was left behind. Nora approached him as if by chance:

"Good morning Doctor Doukas! What a pleasant surprise to see you again! Do you remember me? We've met at the lecture you gave a week ago, and we had a nice chat!"

"Of course I remember you. (He completely forgot her name and barely could remember her face). We had an enjoyable conversation. What brings you to this place?"

"In case you forgot my name, I'll not be surprised. I'm Nora Wilson, and I came around the campus to visit one of my friends who works in the Admission building."

"I'm pleased to meet you again Ms. Wilson, but in case you are looking for the Admission building, it's on the opposite site, at the corner of the alley."

"Thank you for your kindness, but since I'm already here, maybe we can have lunch together, and a nice exchange of a few words. What do you think?"

(He really didn't want her to know what he was thinking!) His answer was lingering over the words he spoke:

"I take my lunch at the cafeteria and I must warn you that the food is not very tasty."

"If you agree, I'll join you with pleasure and promise not to pay much attention to the food."

"I can see that you are very determined, and

therefore, I have to accept your company, and try together the poor menu which I know very well, but which might be disappointing to you."

Cafeteria was just around the corner, and over the meal, they had a casual conversation, without getting into sensitive subjects. Nora did most of the talking, while he kept silent most of the time. She told him how much she liked the beautiful sites of the city, the night-lights, the people, the shopping boutiques, and so on.

"I don't go out very often", he said, "and I must tell you that I don't know the city very well. My work keeps me busy all the time and I don't have the pleasures other people enjoy so much. Also, I don't have any spare time to socialize and be in touch with people who like entertainment and get together in social activities."

"I understand, and I admire you highly for the work you do. Nevertheless, now and then you probably need a break, even if you are not aware of its necessity. Just to make a suggestion, would you like to join me for dinner, let's say tomorrow night? It will be a great pleasure for me, and I'm sure it will be a good moment of relaxation for you. What do you say?"

(This woman won't give up, he thought.)

"You are very convincing, and maybe you're right. I need from time to time a short break. I'll be working until six and after that, we can go to dinner."

"Splendid! I'll pick you up at six, from the front door of the building."

In that night, Philip thought about that new annoyance in his life. He never felt at ease in company of women, since they were very complicated creatures and he never knew what they expected from him. He had a few casual relations without strings attached, and those were enough to fill some gaps in his life. If one of them will happen to be in his way, the same as the others before, will be no different, since he was unwilling to let anyone get closer to him than he wanted.

With these comforting thoughts, he fell asleep, satisfied with his reasoning.

In that night, Nora had a different vision about her future. She decided to go step by step, slowly, and carefully, such as to make him come closer to her, until he will completely surrender to her plans.

The next day, they met in front of the building at six o'clock. It was the beginning of March, the weather was quite pleasant, and only a few patches of snow covered the ground like in a painting.

"Where would you like us to have dinner? Any special place?", she asked.

"Fast food will be fine."

"Well, not like that. Let's say a cozy restaurant where we can talk, have a glass of wine, and good food. What do you say?"

She just didn't want to scare him away, by mentioning an expensive and luxurious place.

"Whatever you like."

The streets were crowded with people looking for a good time, shopping, and entertainment after a long day of work. Nora drove to a place she knew for its excellent service, good food, and a clientele belonging to the middle class. The menu was rich in an assortment of offerings lots of appetizers, main courses, and selection of good wines. "What would you like?", she asked.

"A hamburger with fries."

She looked at him in astonishment. Philip tried to put a smile on his face, and said:

"You look surprised. I eat hamburger every evening at fast food, on my way home; I like it and it became my favorite dish."

"Perhaps you should change to something different this time."

"No, this is fine and if you ask me what I drink, I will tell you that a soda would be what I like. I don't drink alcoholic beverages."

The conversation was lingering, and not even Nora's vivid imagination could help. They talked about the city, the people who worked there making a good living, about the many places where entertainment was at everyone's reach. She talked mostly, while Philip listened and said a few remarks from time to time. After about two hours, they decided to leave, and Nora let him pay since it was a small bill. She drove him home and the evening was over for both, without any promises to see each other again.

A few days went by, and one evening Nora showed up again in front of the building, waiting for Philip to come out.

"I wanted to see you again, and maybe we can have dinner tonight."

"I'm very tired, I had a hard day, and I would like to go home and rest. Your kindness is much appreciated, and maybe tomorrow night we could go out and have dinner."

"Tomorrow it is. I'll pick you up at six."

This time Nora decided to take a different approach. She will take him at the most expensive and luxurious restaurant, and then after, she will take him to her place. If he had to be scared, she will make him to be for the right reason, and that was her big wealth. She called the owner:

"Robert, I'll bring a distinguished guest tomorrow for dinner. Make sure that my table will be ready by six o'clock."

"Yes, Madame, it will be a pleasure to see you."

Nora made sure to be a few minutes late, just to see if Philip cared about their date. He came late too, and apologized. So much for the trick she tried to play on him.

"You look stunning", he said. "Where are we going this time?"

"Thank you for the appreciation. We're going somewhere to eat."

She looked indeed very elegant, her graceful gestures giving her a distinguished way of moving, her barely perceptible smile showing an aristocratic way to please him. A touch of makeup highlighted even more than usual, the regular features of her face, her black hair, and the hazel color of her eyes; she had a slender body, attractive and seductive. Even Philip, who never paid attention at how people looked, was impressed by her appearance.

The restaurant was located on top of the building, and allowed a view of the city from every seat inside. Robert greeted the couple at the entrance and escorted them to the table next to the window, from where the view was magnificent.

"Madame would like to have champagne, before the hors d'oeuvres?"

"Yes, Robert, please."

Two waiters raced each other, to please the guests. They knew how generous that rich woman was, and they didn't want to disappoint her. Robert himself poured the champagne, and watched the service just to make sure that 'Madame' will be pleased as always before. He presented the menu and waited for the order.

"Give us a minute, Robert."

"Certainly, Madame."

Nora wanted to make sure that Philip will not embarrass her by ordering a hamburger this time.

"What is your choice from the menu?"

"Hamburger, but I don't see it listed here."

"They don't serve hamburger here, and maybe you can choose something from what is listed on the menu."

"No offense, but I don't see anything that I like."

She tried not to get upset. With calm and patience, Nora said:

"First will take hors d'oeuvres, and you can choose between soup and a vegetables dish. After that will have the main course, at your choice from the menu, and a dessert. I'll make the choice for you and I'll suggest the *Sole meunière* with steamed potatoes. This is what I'll have; we'll think later about dessert. What do you think?"

"Fine if you say so, but this place is much too expensive and doesn't have a pleasing ambiance", he mumbled.

They dined mostly in silence, now and then saying a few words. Nora thought that what she expected didn't come out, while Philip thought that he had to do something, not to let this imposed relation on him, go any further.

He wanted to pay the bill, even if it was outrageously high, but she didn't let him. They left, and on the way out, Philip said:

"It was quite a pleasant evening and thank you for the invitation. Nevertheless, I must tell that we cannot see each other again. We don't belong to the same league, we have nothing to share, and I'm sure we are not compatible, not even a bit. We've met a few times and I became more convinced that we don't have anything in common. It's just a waste of time for us both, and I hope you'll agree."

"I understand, and maybe you're right, but I don't see any harm to have from time to time a small talk, maybe lunch in a modest place, or a short walk in the park, just to take a break from what we're doing; nothing else, and nothing on regular basis. We'll both consider to be just casual acquaintances, without any strings attached. What do you think?"

"This is acceptable and as you said, there is no harm done, if there is nothing else on the side."

While in the car, Nora said:

"It's still early, about eight o'clock, and just to celebrate our decision, I suggest to stop by my place and have a cup of coffee together. Would be this acceptable?"

"I have class tomorrow morning and I still have to go over some papers, but I can spare a few moments and enjoy a cup of coffee."

He was stunned by the luxury of her place. Everything there was the state of great comfort and extravagant living.

"I'm impressed. You must be very rich, as I can see."

"Very. I inherited a few oil wells in the Permian Basin, next to Midland city, and I share my heritance with my brother who lives there. Money is not everything in life, but makes everything easy."

"I wouldn't know that, since I come from a poor family, working on the farm. I'm the first in three generations who went to school and got an education. It was not easy, but it was rewarding."

"When did you have time to build such an athletic body?"

"I worked on the farm next to my father since I was only six years old. I believe that was a good place to build a strong body. I learned a lot about farming and at a very young age I've already decided to study plant science at a deep level. It became a passion which gave me a great reward."

"Did you have your own farm?"

"I always wished to have one, but never could afford. It would have been a blessing, since I could have experimented with theories developed only under a microscope. Maybe later, one day, I'll be able to have a few acres, with a glass greenhouse and a laboratory where to expand my new findings."

Nora listened very carefully to everything he said, and a new decision sprang up into her mind: she will buy him a farm.

He stayed over night and they came closer without showing each other special feelings or an attitude that promised new attachments.

Next day, Nora flew to Midland. She told her brother everything about Philip, except the agreement between them.

"I want to marry him", she said.

"Did he ask?"

"No, but I will."

"Coming from you, nothing surprises me. Do you love him?"

"No, but I like him enough to marry him, and I believe he likes me too."

"How old is he?"

"Thirty and I'm thirty-two. This is not important."

"What if he refuses? Then you'll get hurt, and I don't want you to suffer. He might very well not want to get married."

"He will. I'll buy him a farm to make his experiments and spend the time he wants on his scientific projects."

"Nora, maybe you know what you're doing, because I don't. Just make sure that you don't get hurt again, like the last time."

"Jack, this is different. Philip is the most noble man I know, beside you, and I'm sure that even without loving each other, we can have a durable and harmonious marriage."

"Are you going to change your name?"

"I'm going to add his name to mine. I'll be called *Nora Wilson Doukas*."

Her brother was a very gentle, generous and considerate man. He was married to Sarah, who was a high school teacher, and they had two very young girls, identical twins, Cora and Alice. The family meant everything in his life and he would do all in his power to protect them. Nora gave him always something to worry about, but he loved her dearly, and he knew that she needed him. He was three years older and when their parents died, he assumed entire responsibility to help her swim safely to the shore. There was a very strong bond between them making them believe that nothing in the world could break it.

"Where do you plan to get married? Do you want me to make all the arrangements to have the ceremony here?"

"No, dearest brother, but thanks for the thought. I don't want him to get scared by our over abundant wealth. We'll make it with a small gathering in a nice place in Austin. You, and Sarah, and the girls are invited."

After about three weeks, Nora left. Her next plan was to find a mid-sized wheat farm, in a good location, coming with equipment and fencing, having water resources, and before anything, to be checked thoroughly by a qualified expert in soil related assets. She hired an Agricultural Real Estate Agent specialized in wheat farmland, who had to follow her instructions to the letter in finding the property she wanted. He showed her several farms quite acceptable, but they were not exactly at her expectation. After a good search, he found the right farm to please her. It was located about ten miles far from Tilden, a small but very rich town not far from Austin; it was the size of around four hundred acres, and had a beautiful mansion, colonial style. The farm needed a few improvements, and some additional small constructions, which could be done later. After the entire area was checked and approved by the soil expert, Nora bought the farm. Before anything else, she needed a knowledgeable foreman to be in charge with the management of the crew workers, the equipment, and the farming process. She asked the agent if he knew someone who could be trusted and capable to do the job.

"It happens that a good foreman had to quit recently his job because he got married and the owner does not accept families on his farm. He came to me looking for a place to work and I promised him to find one. I think he will be the best for you, Ms. Wilson, if you accept him and his wife."

"Children?"

"No, but..."

"Send him to me, and we'll see later about his growing family."

After a couple of days, a very strong, quite tall man, in his thirties, showed up at her apartment in Austin.

"Good morning Ms. Wilson. I'm Joshua Reid and came for the interview regarding the job on your farm."

They talked about two hours. Nora tried not to miss any detail that was of interest to her. He answered to all her questions with honesty, and the interview came out very satisfactory for both of them.

"When can I see the farm?", he asked.

"We can go now, and if you have a car, you can follow me."

Arrived there, Joshua looked around, making notes about everything he considered to be mentioned. He made a long list comprising improvements to the buildings and especially the changes to be made regarding the machinery inventory. After finishing, he talked to Nora, showing her the observations he made and giving her the list with his suggestions.

"Mr. Reid, since I hired you as a manager of this place, I trust your judgment. Do everything you mentioned there on paper, and bring me the bill. You also, hire the crew you need to help you starting the work on this farm. In the meantime, I'll contact a reliable construction company, to build an addition to the house, and a glass greenhouse on the side. You will also be in charge with the supervision of the contractor's work and inform me about its progress. I'll also change the entire furniture in the main house. You know where to find me, for all you need, or I have to know. You are in charge, and I hope that everything will be a smooth endeavor, without any problems. You can move anytime in the building assigned to you and your wife. Good day."

In the meantime, in those almost four weeks since they didn't see each other, Philip was busy with his class and worked hard in his laboratory at one new theory about the *endosperm* of the wheat, expecting to find a new way of increasing the stored energy in the seed. He completely forgot about Nora, and only from time to time, he remembered bits of their conversation, being content that she was not around.

One evening, Nora called Philip. He was in a conference, and she didn't leave a message. The next day, she called him again and asked him to join her for dinner.

"We haven't seen each other in quite a long time", she said when he showed up at the front of the building. "I missed you."

He didn't say that he missed her also, because it would have been a lie.

"I don't have much time, but we can grab a bite somewhere, since we both have to eat."

He asked her what she did lately, just to make conversation, and not because he was curious. She told him very little from her busy schedule and from the plans she succeeded so well to achieve.

"Let me drive you home, and maybe I can stay overnight", she said.

(This woman is pushing, and pushing me again, and again, he thought.)

"My place is in shambles. I never have time to

clean it, and actually I don't need to do it, since I can find my way around very easy."

"Listen Philip, you think that I'll judge you for that? I'm not interested a bit, in how your place looks like. I just want to spend a little time with you. Would this be so hard for you?"

"No, but I don't feel comfortable. Anyway, if you insist, let's go to my place", he mumbled.

His place was indeed in shambles as he said, but she spent the night, waiting for a right moment to approach a more sensitive subject. He woke up early in the morning, and was ready to leave, when she asked:

"Will you marry me?"

He was stunned, like being struck by lightening. This time he gave up the fragile cover of politeness, which being ruled only by his annoyance, was ready to break at any time.

"Are you out of your mind? Have you lost all your senses? I don't love you, and you don't love me, which means that the main ingredient used in a marriage is totally missing between us. We are not compatible at all, and the only communication between us, is a small talk over a meal, from time to time. Isn't this enough for you? For me, this is more than enough, and more than I can handle in this so called 'relation'. Put your mind back in your head, if ever you had one, and leave me alone with my life the way it is."

Nora expected a civilized refusal, against

which she intended to fight, but never she expected such rudeness. She composed herself, trying to have a dignified attitude:

"You treated me like trash, and I don't deserve this. I'll leave you alone with your life the way it is, as you said, and promise not to bother and not to see you ever again."

She run outside and burst into tears. On her way home, she sobbed like never before, thinking that no one ever made her cry like that.

In the next day, Nora called Joshua who said that the project was going according to schedule and in less than a month everything will be ready. She flew to Midland to recover from the difficult condition she was going through, and once there, she told everything to her brother. He was her best friend, her counselor, her protector, and he knew her better than anyone else.

"That professor doctor scientist, big mind, or whatever, who searches to improve the way of life, is nothing but a jerk and a specimen of low life himself. What are you going to do with the farm, now?"

"I don't have any idea. I would like to keep it for a while, and then I might sell it. You know Jack, I fell in love with that place, for its natural beauty, for the way I could listen to silence, and for the many new things I've learned there. I wish you could see it."

"You have time to decide. For now, have a good rest, and stay home until you'll feel better."

"Don't tell Sarah about my problems."

"I never do. She has enough work to deal with, and doesn't need to have more worries than she can handle."

Nora spent her time mostly resting and trying to put her thoughts together. She loved her home where she grew up with her family and where she always felt safe. Around the house, her mother used to plant and grow a species of small shrub called *Lantana,* which gave beautiful flowers with colors changing from yellow,to orange, and then to red. It was a tender perennial, which grew and multiplied, covering an extended area. Memories of those times overcame her with feelings of nostalgia for the past, when she was happy and had no worries.

Meantime, Philip tried to focus his mental efforts on his work. He just wrote a paper about the *phytochemicals in the wheat grain,* specifically about the *phenolic acids,* which proved to have a number of health benefits. It seemed to be a long time since he saw Nora, and she kept her promise not to bother him anymore. In his humble dwelling, before going to sleep, her last image came from time to time before his eyes. He thought that indeed, he treated her like trash, and somehow he felt guilty and displeased with himself. She was annoying him, all right, but never did harm to him.

Her proposal to marriage infuriated him enough to make him say those cruel words he otherwise wouldn't even think about.

(I owe her an apology and I'll tell her that I'm sorry, he said to himself.)

Philip didn't know her phone number, since he never asked for it, and never intended to call her. He decided to go by her place and apologize in person.

"Ms. Wilson left town and didn't say when she will be back", the door attendant told him.

Philip thought that perhaps a short note of apology will be appropriate. He wrote just a few words: "I'm sorry and apologize for my behavior." The next day, he gave the envelope and a big tip to the door attendant.

"Your name, Sir?"

"Ms. Wilson knows me."

He felt some kind of relief, but still the feeling of guilt didn't seem to diminish. He thought that after all, Nora was the only person who called him, liked talking to him, and was interested in his life. His relations with his colleagues were strictly professional, and no one of them cared about his personal life, or called him just to ask him for a chat or to have dinner together. A feeling of loss gripped him, without actually making him aware that he wished her to call him like before. He realized that his life came across a particular experience since he met her, and many new feelings appeared like suddenly, never encountered by him before. Nevertheless, it was too late, and probably he will never see her again.

Nora, in the meantime, stayed in touch almost every other day with Joshua who kept her up to date about the progress of the project. After about one month, he gave her the good news:

"Everything is ready and came out very well."

She told her brother and asked him:

"Can you spare a few days and come with me to see the farm?"

"I certainly can and I'll be happy to accompany you, my little, dear sister."

In the coming weekend, they flew to Austin. Nora got the note from Philip and showed it to Jack.

"He is still a jerk, but now a polite one", he said, "are you going to call him?"

"No. It took me some time to recover, and I don't want to go again through the same experience. Tomorrow morning we'll go see the farm."

It took them about three hours to get there. Nora stopped the car in front of the iron-forged portal, which was indeed a beautiful art work. On top was written the word *LANTANA* with arched letters.

"This is the name of our mother's favorite flower!" Jack shouted.

"I chose it in remembrance of her and of the wonderful time we had together."

"That's very thoughtful, Nora, and I like the idea."

She drove on the narrow country road leading to the mansion and stopped the car in front of door.

"Is this a farm house?", Jack asked in amazement. "It looks like our mansion back home in Midland!"

"It is a mansion, a little smaller than the one we have home. Let's get inside and don't stand there like a boulder!"

The inside of the house amazed Jack even more. It looked exquisite.

"How much did you pay for this?"

"It's not your money."

"Just curious. It must be a fortune!"

Everything was indeed beautiful, of excellent quality and taste.

"Is there any food in this house? I'm hungry."

"You had a big breakfast this morning, and no, there is no food in this house, since I don't live here."

"Maybe those people who work for you, have something to eat."

"Aren't you ashamed at all?"

"No. Just hungry."

Nora called Joshua on the phone and asked him to come over. After only a few minutes, he showed up at the back door, accompanied by his wife. They both carried some plates with cookies and a coffee pot. She smiled and put everything on the kitchen table.

"Mrs. and Mr. Wilson, this is my wife, Mya."

"I'm pleased to finally meet you Mrs. Reid. I'm Nora Wilson and this is my brother, Jack. I see you brought us some goodies and coffee. Thank you and let's all have a seat."

"I'm likewise, very pleased to meet you Ms. Wilson. I baked this cookies this morning, knowing that you had to come, and must be hungry after such a long drive."

She was very charming, with nice features, blond reddish hair combed into a small bun, green eyes and a very pleasing smile. After they all enjoyed some cookies and a cup of coffee, Joshua suggested going and inspecting the farm.

"I'll leave you now, and wish you a pleasant tour of the farm. I had to go and cook for the workers who always have a big appetite. I'll make today for them, beef stew with veggies and steamed potatoes, which they mostly like. Good day, Ms. Wilson and Mr. Wilson."

"Good day, Mrs. Reid", they both answered.

It was a sunny day, and a gentle breeze whispering over the wide-open land made the whole field look alive.

While inspecting the farm, Nora and Jack were in a continuous amazement. Everything there stimulated a great pleasure to see, and proved the best work that could be accomplished and paid with big money.

The newly attached building, which had a communication door with the main house, was exactly what Nora wanted. It had two rooms with all the amenities, and one of the doors opened into the glass greenhouse, adjacent to it, and which was amazingly well built, having heat and irrigation systems of the most modern technology. Two sides of it were completely closed, while the third one had a door opening into an area of about ten acres of land, all fenced.

"I'm impressed, Mr. Reid", Nora said, "I've anticipated a good job, but this is above my expectations, to the smallest details. Congratulations for everything you realized here."

"Thank you Ms. Wilson, I just did the job you told me to do, and for which I was well paid. Now, if there is nothing else I can do for you, I have to take care of the field and of my crew. We did the spring planting. It is a good year and I expect a very good yield in fall. It is a small area on the West site where perennial wheat grew from last year and has to be harvested. We'll do it soon. If there will be something unexpected that needs your attention, I'll call you. Good day Ms.Wilson, Mr. Wilson."

"I am in ecstasy", Jack said, "sell the farm to me. I'll double the price you paid for everything. This is the best place for the family, to spend a vacation and have a great time. What do you think?"

"I don't sell it, Jack. I'll keep the farm for myself, but the family is always welcome to come here anytime, have a vacation, great time, and enjoy the fresh air, which doesn't smell oil and gas."

They returned to town, and Jack wanted to do some shopping for the family. It was Sunday still early afternoon, and they had plenty of time to walk around and have a good time.

"Let's go eat first", he said, "I'm hungry."

"You're always hungry. Where do you want us to go, and what would be your pleasure today?"

"I would like to have beef stew with veggies and steamed potatoes."

"Looks like Mya inspired your huge appetite. This kind of dish can be found only in a diner and not in a select restaurant. Let's go see, and maybe you get lucky."

Inside the diner, a corpulent woman greeted them with a smile and said that she just cooked that dish, freshly in the morning.

"It's sooooo good", Jack said, "I can eat this everyday. Why back home our cook never makes it?"

Nora was amused, but she also liked that meal, which indeed was excellent.

They left very satisfied, and went to a bookstore, bought some children books for the girls, and Jack was looking for something special to give Sarah.

"She always wanted to have a *Larousse*", he said "and never could find one."

"We can try the antique bookstore which is not far from here. Let's go there and find out."

Once inside, Jack asked the bookstore clerk about a later edition of a *Larousse.* It so happened that he had only one volume, in a very good shape, but it was expensive. Actually, it was a bargain for its worth.

At the science section, a man perused a book when he heard a voice he recognized only very well. He turned his head and saw the couple who talked with the clerk. A distressing thought suddenly crossed his mind:

(She didn't waste time to replace me, he said to himself. I don't feel guilty anymore.)

An urge to humiliate that woman seized him, and he already prepared some harsh words to say to her. Philip felt his anger seize him, and made a few steps approaching the couple who were ready to leave. Nora heard his voice behind her and froze:

"Nice to see you again, Ms. Wilson. I didn't think that this place would be your choice for entertainment."

"Doctor Doukas, I didn't expect to see you, so soon. This is my brother, Jack Wilson. Jack, this is Doctor Doukas, an old acquaintance."

It was Philip's turn to freeze. He only could whisper:

"I'm pleased to meet you Mr. Wilson."

Philip stretched his hand, but Jack didn't take it. He only said:

"Hello," and then addressed his sister:

"Let's go, Nora, it's getting late."

She only said:

"Good bye, Doctor Doukas."

Without any other words, they turned around and left.

Once outside, Jack asked:

"This is the jerk who made your life a mess?"

"Yes, Jack, and please let's not talk about him. Let's go and see a fashion boutique. I want to buy something nice for Sarah."

Late evening they went home and talked a lot about the good time spent together, and not a word about Philip.

Next day, Jack flew home to Midland. Before going to the airport, he asked:

"What are you going to do now?"

"I'll stay for a while at the farm, learning a little bit about growing wheat, knowing my people there, and breathing the fresh air. Further than that I don't know what to tell. I'm taking step by step and this is a safe way to live peacefully. I'll come home after a month or so, and stay there for a while. Maybe later, I'll take a job as a consultant on call and not on permanent basis with a business investing firm. Maybe, but for now, I don't know what else to tell you. Give a kiss to everybody out there."

They hugged each other, and Jack left.

After a couple of days, Nora packed her car with casual clothing, pants, overalls, shorts, and boots. She also bought a big supply of food to last for at least a month, and then she started her trip, heading to the farm. In the coming weeks, she learned more about the farm, the people working there, and about the entire surrounding that incited new feelings unknown to her until then.

In the meantime, Philip's last paper was conferred with a special award in recognition for its merit. Also, a grant was bestowed upon him, for a new project of research. Philip was only thirty years old, but already recognized as one of the most gifted scientists in his generation. He was on his way up to fame probably, but his personal life was a mess. When he saw Nora at the bookstore and knew that her companion was her brother, he felt ashamed, guilty, and abandoned. In the past few months, he felt like missing her more, especially her smile and her lot of talking about everything coming to her mind, which was of little or none interest to him. He never could believe that one day he will miss her so much. He wanted her back. How will he feel if she wouldn't forgive him and she wouldn't come back to him? He didn't find an answer, and actually, he didn't even want to think about such a failure.

One evening he went to her apartment and found out from the door attendant that she was out of town, and didn't say when she will be back. Philip gave him a big tip and his phone number:

"When she comes back, call me", he said.

He went home and in that evening, he couldn't concentrate on his work. His thoughts were swirling in his mind and his feelings were all confused. He only could wait and see what will come next.

After a while, he received a call from the door attendant, telling him that Ms. Wilson was back. It was around seven o'clock in that evening when Philip showed at her apartment. Nora opened the door and was stunned when she saw him. Without any words, he took her in his arms and kissed her passionately.

"Marry me", he whispered.

"Do you love me?"

"I don't really know what love for a woman is, but I feel better being with you, and I feel worse being without you. I know the difference and I think this must be love."

"It's a start. I'm captivated by your definition of love. I'll marry you."

He was thrilled. The next day, Nora called her brother and told him the news.

"Why am I not surprised?", Jack asked, "Make sure that you'll not be hurt again by that jerk."

"I won't. He is the man I want in my life."

In the coming weekend they got married,

having a small ceremony attended only by Nora's few friends and Philip's four colleagues.

It was summer time already and vacation for school. They didn't decide yet where to live, and needed a little time to choose. Nora asked:

"Would you like us to have a small honeymoon, somewhere in a peaceful place, to relax and maybe knowing better each other?"

"Yes, very much. Where?"

"I know a beautiful place, with fresh air and a peaceful surrounding. Trust me, you'll like it."

"I don't appreciate surprises, but since we are freshly married, I'll go with your choice."

Next morning, they headed to the farm. Over the almost three hours of drive, they talked about their new way of life, hoping in good faith that their marriage will work well. Nora stopped the car at Tilden, and bought supply food to last for a little while.

"There is no restaurant in that place, where we can eat?"

"Not really, and it's better for us to be prepared."

It took them about ten minutes to arrive at the farm, and Nora stopped the car in front of the portal.

"LANTANA?!", Philip exclaimed, "this is a beautiful shrub flower which is perennial and grows a little North from here."

"Really? It's very interesting."

She drove to the mansion and stopped the car

in front of the main door. Philip stepped out and looked around in amazement.

"This is a farm, Nora!"

"Very good, Philip! This is indeed a farm, and it's ours; yours and mine."

The man with feelings of steel, who never allowed himself to have weaknesses, had tears in his eyes that he could not control running down his face. Nora embraced him and said like whispering:

"I too, have my own definition of love. Let's get inside and see our new house."

Philip looked around like in a dream. He never saw in his life such a splendid place.

"Is this a house where we can live?"

Nora had a short laugh, and said:

"That's what they call it. The word is usually in dictionaries and is described in multiple ways."

"I'm speechless. I don't know what to say. I feel like I'm dreaming. Is everything around for real, Nora?"

"I suppose so. I'll call now the manager and you both certainly will have a lot to talk."

Joshua was in the field but it took him only few minutes to come. Nora made the presentations and told him that her husband knows a lot about farming and he is eager to see the farm.

"We are very busy now in the field, but I'll leave instructions to my crew and you can accompany me. I'll be happy to show you everything around,

Doctor Doukas. You'll need special clothing, which I can provide for you. Are you ready?"

"More than I ever was."

It was close to noon time when they left. Nora called Mya and asked if she could spare a little time and come over. She told her about getting married last week, and wanted to learn how to cook hamburgers for her husband. Mya was happy to show her the best recipe and Nora learned very quickly and made no mistakes. She waited for Philip to come back and see amazement on his face, when he'll have his favorite meal. He returned to the house late, after six, when the working day was over, and Joshua became tired of showing him around and of talking with him the most notable facts about farming, that they both shared with big interest.

"I'll work with you and the crew tomorrow all day long, and we'll talk again. Good night, Joshua."

"Good night, Philip. I've never anticipated to have so much pleasure like I had today when I've learned a lot from you. I'll see you tomorrow."

"Are you hungry?", Nora asked.

"No. I'm still in a state of amazement and it's hard for me to believe that I'll be able to work in the laboratory on this farm. Joshua is very knowledgeable, very friendly, I like him a lot, and we call each other by our first names. Tomorrow, I'll climb on the combine and harvest the crop still in the small areas on the West site, where it was planted to regrow like perennial wheat. I intend to seed in those areas a variety of wheat with a stronger kernel."

Nora kept looking at him, without saying a word. He was in his beloved world, and she couldn't be part of it.

Early in the morning, he woke up and was ready to go to the field. Nora gave him a hearty breakfast and he said:

"I'll be back in the evening. What are you going to do today?"

"I'll find something."

He left and she planned without any enthusiasm to go out, to Tilden, buy some farm clothing for Philip, buy some flower seeds to plant in front of the house, and some herbs seeds for the back. At least she had something to do with her time. In that day she also went to a Household Agency and hired a cook by the name Betty, and a housekeeper named Irene, who also will have the assignment to serve at the table. They both had to start their job in the coming week.

Philip came late, hungry, and tired.

"I finished the work on that site, and I'm satisfied. It is a long time since I climbed on a combine, but I feel like it was yesterday. What did you do today?"

She told him, without showing much enthusiasm, but saying that it was a good time to spend.

"I would like to ask a favor", he said. "Now, that I finished for the time being the work in the field, I want to start my research project in the lab. For this, I need to have my equipment from my apartment, and I need you to drive me there. Would you?"

"Of course. We can go any time, maybe tomorrow morning."

Next day they went to Austin, he took his equipment, books, and some belongings. They spent the day in town, trying to have a good time, and avoiding to talk about their sensitive feelings for one another. They went to her apartment, she took some of her stuff, pictures of her family, her computer, her music recorder and tapes, then they went shopping for some things needed for the household. When ready to go back to the farm, he took his car and followed her. Late night they arrived home, were tired, and went directly to sleep.

Summer was almost gone, the school year was about to start, and around September 1st Joshua will begin harvesting the spring wheat planted in April.

"In a week I have to go back to teaching. This year I'll have four classes, but I'll schedule them Monday and Tuesday, and stay in my apartment; I'll be home for the rest of the week, working on my projects. One of my students who works for his Doctoral Degree under my supervision, will be available to be my assistant and help me here in the lab. Nevertheless, I need your consent to hire him, since he needs boarding, that means food and a place to sleep. May I have your consent, Nora?"

"Of course. He can sleep in one of the rooms next to your lab, and there is plenty of food in the house."

"I'll bring him next week when I'll come home. His name is James, he is a very quiet man, very kind, and…."

"I'm pregnant."

Philip jumped and took her in his arms, kissing her again, and again.

"You make me the happiest man in this entire world, Nora! This news is wonderful! Can you imagine to have a child who is part of ourselves and who will be the strongest bond between us! This is a miracle!"

She looked at him and only said:

"This was an accident. I don't want this child. I don't think I could be a good mother. Besides, I don't have patience to raise him. I'll seek to have an abortion, whether you like it or not."

"Nora, look at me. This is something new for you and you are scared. Try not to be. I'll be always next to you, helping with everything I can. Don't do something that you'll regret for the rest of your life and feel guilty about, every single day of your life. We can hire a skilled nanny who will take care of the baby, and you'll see, he will grow up in no time. He will be the greatest joy and a blessing for us both. Think about the happiness that child could bring us and the light he will shine upon us. Think about, Nora, think."

"Maybe on the surface, you're right, Philip. I guess I'm just scared to give birth first, and then after to take responsibility of raising a child, with all the care for his health, education, behavior, and so on."

"We'll do it together, and you'll see, we'll raise a prince or a princess of honorable character and of intellectual elite."

She came close to him and whispered:

"Hold me tightly and never let me go."

Philip decided to keep an eye on her to make sure that she will not do something to end the pregnancy. He also asked the house staff to be careful all the time around her and watch that she will not get hurt. If she needed to go to town, one of the staff will accompany her and do the driving, without leaving her alone, not for a moment. He started the school as scheduled, but was worried all the time, especially when he had to stay in town over night. In the following week, he brought home with him, his assistant James, showed him around, and put him in charge with parts of his project regarding Plant Metabolism and Chemodiversity.

Joshua started harvesting the wheat planted in spring, and after that he will begin to plant the winter wheat, which will need about seven to eight months to grow.

Nora and Philip seemed to get closer to one another, even if only because he cared all the time more about his coming child than about her, but she didn't suspect anything like that. So far, the path of their life was no longer into the wind.

Nora called her brother and told him the news. He was overjoyed and asked her to take care of herself and not to do anything foolish.

It was already the end of October, and as expected, the wheat yield was huge. The market was very good and the sale brought a remarkable profit. Every worker on the farm received a substantial bonus, and Joshua was rewarded with ten percent of the gain. Mya was thrilled.

"This is wonderful, Josh! If we can save money like this, a few more years from now, we can buy our place and start our family!"

"We can do that, Mya. For now, we'll start saving and spend only little money from time to time for small things just to please us."

The month of December was already there, and snow was covering the fields like a blanket of protection for the planted seeds. All the farm workers went home to their families in the villages nearby. Schools were closed, Christmas vacation started, and everybody was more relaxed. James didn't go on vacation and chose to stay close to Philip and work on the project. The green house was full with new, very young plants, grown from seeds with different traits elaborated under the microscope, and which indicated a scientific proof of a new theory. Now and then, Joshua joined them, to learn, to watch, and to help. From time to time, Philip checked on Nora, making sure that she was all right.

"Would you like to invite some of your friends for Christmas dinner?", he asked.

"No. We don't need that."

"I thought, maybe you'll like to have them around and spend a good time together."

"I said, no! I don't want them to see my deformed body."

With every passing day, she became more gloomy and taciturn. Philip was very worried, but he had nobody to talk about or ask someone for an advice. He just needed to watch her more carefully, and had to leave James to take care of the experiments.

A few days before Christmas, James drove to town and bought a spruce tree and ornaments. He placed it in the main hall, next to the piano and started decorating when Nora saw him:

"What is this doing here?"

"I thought a Christmas tree would be nice to have for the holiday, Nora."

"Why didn't you ask before? I don't have need for that and I don't have time to decorate it."

"I'll do that. Gives me great pleasure, and reminds me of my home."

She didn't say another word and left.

Before Christmas dinner, Philip asked her:

"Wouldn't be nice to invite Joshua and Mya? They are alone and have nobody to share the Christmas meal. What do you think?"

"How about Betty and Irene? They don't have anybody either. Are you inviting them also? Maybe I should serve you all at the table!"

"You know something Nora? I'm sick and tired pampering you all the time, making sure that you are well and comfortable. Yes, I'll invite them all, and have a good time, for a change."

"Then, I'll not be part of your gathering. I'll stay in my room, and don't come to pamper me!"

Philip did what he said. The entire staff was there and he told them about his wife's condition; she was not feeling well, and wanted to have a rest. They all had a tremendous time, telling jokes and stories, singing Christmas carols, and feeling like in family. From time to time, Mya or Betty checked on Nora, but she was asleep, or maybe she pretended to be asleep. Anyway, she seemed to be all right.

She woke up late in the morning and asked about the party.

"We had a very good time", Philip said, "come with me."

He took her by the hand and went to the main

hall, where all the others were there, next to the tree, as Philip asked them to come.

"Merry Christmas everybody! Thank you all for the good work and for your loyalty."

He gave to each one of them an envelope with a check with the same amount of money. To Nora he gave a small jewelry box. She opened it and was amazed. There was a round pendant with a diamond on a gold chain.

"Thank you, Philip. It's beautiful, and I'll wear it from time to time."

She was touched and changed her mood for a moment.

"Merry Christmas, my dear. I'm glad you like it."

"But we don't have a present for you", one of them said."

"You all are the best present for me. I don't need anything else."

The month of April was already there, and by the end of it, Nora gave birth to a beautiful baby boy. At the hospital, the nurse showed him to her, but Nora didn't want to touch him. She only had a big sigh and closed her eyes. Philip took the baby in his arms and whispered:

"He is the miracle in my life. Look at him, Nora. I've already fell in love with him."

She didn't even want to look at her baby.

"She will get over this", the nurse said, "it

happens to many mothers to feel like that. Don't worry."

Philip hired a skilled nanny, who also was registered nurse, recommended by his friend, a Pediatrician Doctor. Her name was Rachel West, she was around forty years old, short, plump, had quick moves, and lived alone.

While Nora was in the hospital, Philip, James, and Mya, prepared the nursery for the baby and an adjacent room for the nanny, with all the furniture and everything was mentioned in the books.

After a week, Philip brought Nora home, with the baby and the nanny.

"How do you want to call him?", Philip asked.

"It's yours; you give him the name you want, because I really don't care."

The baby was born on Sunday and Philip gave him the Greek name *Matheo,* after his father. The meaning of it was "Gift of God."

Every late evening, Philip went to the nursery, sat on a chair next to the crib, looking at his baby, and whispering an old Greek lullaby learned from his mother. His feeling of love deep buried in his soul long time ago, surfaced up in its entire splendor, with the birth of his son. He never had a feeling alike. That baby was part of him, part of what he was, he felt, he thought, he lived. It was a miracle that brought a blessing light over the path of his life.

Philip could only stay a few minutes there, only

that long as Rachel allowed him to stay. She was very categorical and exigent in everything she did; she wore a white coat, a cap, and a face mask, and not allowed anyone to come near to the baby. She also asked for a bed to be put in the nursery, so she could be day and night close to him. Philip learned all her rules, and never stepped on them. He was extremely pleased with the care Rachel had for the baby, especially that Nora didn't want to come close to him, refused to breastfeed him, and was not even curious to see her child.

Philip was getting more and more worried. What will happen if Nora neglects the child and does not give up her stubbornness to not even get close to him? Didn't she have maternal instincts at all? How will Philip raise his child without a mother whom the child knows lives in the same house and who had no feeling of love for him? Questions after questions swirled in Philip's mind without being able to find an answer to even one of them. He thought that maybe later the future would become even darker, if Nora might have a hostile attitude toward the child who had to grow up in a harmonious atmosphere in order to develop at a fragile age when the character is formed and when the mind needs the richness of the first teachings of behavior. Then, the child will react naturally, adopting an antagonistic attitude toward his own mother, and will continue to form with deformities in character that will gradually accentuate with increasing age and will manifest toward those who will be in his life. He will become a disappointed adult who could easily use uncontrolled abuse and violence. Philip needed the advice of a specialist and decided to consult the doctor who performed Matheo's birth. As explicitly as possible, the doctor talked to him about what is called "baby blues" that affect mothers who have irritability and anxiety starting with the first days after birth. These symptoms may be related to hormonal changes, but may go away within a week or two. More serious and lasting is a condition called "postpartum depression," which causes mood swings, guilt, sadness, and persistent depression, and can be diagnosed up to one year after birth. In these cases, mothers need medication, usually a mood stabilizer and an antipsychotic, for a year before reducing them. Philip understood everything the doctor explained to him, but instead of being calmer, he became even more worried. Nora was not a woman who could easily accept advice or change in attitude. How will he succeed in convincing her of the need for medical treatment and make her accept that her condition is serious and cannot be neglected while waiting to pass by itself? It was a question to which the doctor had only one answer: "with great patience and calm."

Philip called Nora and told her that they have to talk.

"About what?"

"About your condition that seems to worsen."

He told her everything in details the doctor explained him, saying that she needs medical attention and take the prescription indicated by the doctor.

Nora started yelling like mad:

"I don't need medical treatment! You need! You neglected me completely since I've gave birth to that child! You don't even know anymore that I exist! He stole your love for me! You're only concerned about him, and not a bit about me! Can your doctor give me a pill to love that child, because I don't have any love for him! Go to hell with your medical treatment and take your child with you! I don't need either of you!"

Philip was stunned.

"Nora, you're wrong. Love has different way to be given and each of you has its part of my love which is plenty for both. You're confused now and have to understand that Matheo needs both his parents to be raised and cherished and protected. He has to grow up in a loving climate where you and I would be around him all the time. For now, until you get better I'll take care of him with the help of his nanny; you need medical treatment because your actual condition might get worse. Please listen to me and let's help each other to get together over this crisis. Please, Nora."

"You said everything, and so did I!"

She turned around and left, slamming the door. Philip had a big sigh, thinking that there was nothing left for him to do, but only taking care of his child and making sure that she will not hurt him.

Their path of life was again into the wind.

Meantime, Joshua started harvesting the crop planted in winter, and after that, he planted the spring wheat. By the end of May, Nora flew to Midland, with hope that she might get rid of her bitterness.

She told her brother about her feeling of great distress.

"I'm no material for mother. That child stole Philip's love for me, and now he doesn't care about me anymore."

Jack became irritated:

"Did you hear what you just said? How can you be so foolish? A child is the strongest bond between two people. I adore my children, and this makes me love even more my wife. It's a different kind of love that one feels and gives. You always thought only about yourself, your needs, your pleasures, your exciting life, and never cared what other people feel, think, or do. It's time to change and become a more unselfish and considerate person. Go home girl, put your act together, and bring your senses to normal; talk to Philip. He must be a good man if he can deal with a spoiled minx like you. Go home to him and together you'll build a beautiful and strong family."

After two weeks, Nora returned home. She was determined to end the turbulent crisis she went through, one-step at the time. It was Monday, Philip had classes, and he won't be back until Wednesday. James also was in town, working on his thesis. Nora went to the nursery, opened the door, and slowly stepped inside. Rachel was reading a book, while the baby was sleeping. He was already six weeks old, and that was the first time when she was so close to him. She looked at him and felt like astonishment grew more and more on her face. She could whisper only that loud as to be heard by the nanny:

"He is a miniature replica of his father."

"Yes, he looks like him, only at a smaller scale," Rachel commented. "Would you like to sit down, Mrs. Doukas?"

"Just for a few moments. Can he see and hear?"

"A newborn can only focus about eight to twelve inches from his face, and he sees only black, white, and gray. As the months go by, he will slowly start to develop his color vision at around four months. As for hearing, a newborn has been hearing sounds since way back in the womb, like his mother heartbeat, the gurgles of her digestive system, and even the sounds of her voice. Once he is born, the sounds of the outside world come in loud and clear. The most amazing feature he develops is his smile, which you can notice every time you speak or sing to him. Every evening his father comes to see him, sits on this chair and sings him a lullaby. Even if he is asleep, he shows a smile on his face. He already recognizes the voice of his father and smiles every time he hears it."

"This is amazing, indeed. Thank you Ms. West for sharing with me your knowledge. Good night."

"Good night Mrs. Doukas."

Before going home Wednesday morning, Philip went to the bank and opened a living trust fund account for Matheo, which only he could access when he will be twenty-one years old. Somehow, Philip had a feeling of relief, thinking that his son will be secure until he will have a job to support himself. After that, he went home, directly to his lab to drop his papers and wash up before seeing his son. Nora was in the greenhouse looking at the variety of plants.

"What are you doing here?", he asked.

"Admiring your garden. These are the new experiments? Are they better than the ones they are coming from?"

"Some are better, some need improvement, and more study. We planted many of them outside and we'll see how they develop on an extended area. How was your vacation?"

"It was not a vacation. I just needed some time alone to clear up my mind trying to get over my crisis. I saw the baby, and the nanny explained me a lot of things about newborns that I didn't know. He looks like you, like being your miniature replica."

She took a long look at him, not saying another word. He was even more handsome, seemingly with other passing day. He had a glow on his face like never before.

"What are you staring at?"

"Just thinking how much you two look alike. It's amazing."

"Did you hold him?"

"No."

Philip didn't ask any more questions, because he didn't want to find out her feelings.

He tried to have a mild tone when saying:

"I'm going to see my son. Would you like to come, or you have better things to do?"

"I'm coming with you."

The nanny was feeding the baby when they came in.

"Good morning, Rachel, how is my boy doing today?"

She answered to him, not paying any attention to Nora:

"Good morning Philip, he is marvelous and hungry as usually. He can hold his bottle and cooing from time to time as showing a great pleasure. I'm taking him outside for a bit of fresh air and enjoying the sunny day. Would you like to accompany us, Mrs. Doukas?"

"No. You're doing a very good job, Ms. West."

Philip had a piercing look in his eyes, but didn't say a word.

Time went by like flying, month after month. The relation between Philip and Nora was on a platform of tolerating each other and the love both expected to become a strong bond, never came between them. Philip adored his son, watching his every step of growing up, while Nora tried to come between them by playing a resolute mother who believed in strong discipline and obedience. Matheo was already one year old, he was extremely attached to his father whom he called "Daddy", and to his nanny whom he called "Nana", while he always was reluctant every time his mother approached or addressed him. He never called her "Mother" or "Mom", but only by her name. He called himself "Mat". Every time he felt pleasure, he smiled and touched his chin, like caressing it. That was a gesture Philip's father had, and somehow, Matheo inherited it. Philip decided not ever to tell his son why Nora neglected him when he was born and even later. If he ever asks, Philip will tell him that his mother was very sick. He just didn't want Matheo to hate her, and to carry in his soul for his entire life the ugliest, the worst, and the most destructive feeling one can have.

Meantime, James earned his doctoral degree and became Assistant Professor at the university. Philip worked alone for his research projects, keeping in the same time his job as professor. His research on Molecular Biology and Genetics and his epidemiological studies, which brought big improvements in selected plants, received an enthusiastic approval in the scientific community and outside.

In the beginning of May, a baby girl was born to Mya and Joshua. By that time, Joshua was about thirty-two years old and Mya was twenty-seven. The baby was born on Sunday and they named her "Alma", which had the meaning of "Nurturing Soul". She was adorable, and only after few weeks, her traits became more contoured, but she seemed not to resemble any of her parents. She was just oneself, with golden blond hair, narrow shaped and hooded eyes of dark green color, long eyelashes, and fair complexion. Both Mya and Joshua adored her, competing with each other to hold and hug her.

Philip and Rachel congratulated them and bought some presents, while Nora only said:

"Good luck!"

The wheat planted in fall grew over the winter and was ready to be harvested. Joshua worked most of the day in the field, while Mya had to take care of the baby and in the same time to prepare the meals for the crew. It was not easy for her, but she managed very well to do both jobs.

Summer was already there, and Philip had two months vacation, intending to spend his time between the lab and his son. Now and then, Nora went to her apartment in town and had a party with her friends, trying not to stay more than a week. She just needed to relax from the tension she went through while adjusting to the ambience in her home. Every day, Philip took Mat on his lap and read him children picture books, teaching him new words and asking him to repeat. He also introduced him to Greek language, with few easy words to pronounce. Mat learned a lot and had a rich vocabulary for his age. It was summer time, the weather was pleasant, and Nana took Mat every day for a walk outside. Philip joined them sometimes, watching his son running, and enjoying every minute of being in company of his father. Nana was not very talkative, but she also liked when Philip had time and joined them outside. She told him that long ago she was married, the marriage didn't work, and she had a daughter who died at a young age. Ever since, she devoted her time to raise children and became a registered nurse and a nanny. Philip liked her a lot, and was happy to have her around and taking such good care of Mat.

Time went by, month after month, year after year. Mat was already five years old, and Alma was four. He was enrolled in kindergarten and she went to preschool. Beside the curriculum, they both will learn how to socialize, share, and contribute to circle time. Mat also, could master quite well a simple conversation in Greek language, which made Philip extremely pleased. Nana drove them to school in Tilden every day and took them home after three hours. She waited in a hall reading a book or knitting while the kids were in class. On their way back, both raced to tell each other about their learning, their teacher, and their classmates. Nana didn't bother to ask any question, because they answered to all of them. After only few weeks, Philip was extremely pleased with the learning program and progress of his son. So were Mya and Joshua when Alma showed them the interesting subjects she learned, and told them about her classmates and her teacher, how nice they were.

When not in school, Mat and Alma used to play a lot outside and be together most of the time. They had a special place where they played, on the right site of the field, where a gigantic *Live Oak Tree* was an impressive sight for that landscape. The tree was reaching about eighty feet in height with about one hundred spread, with many sinuously curved trunks and branches. It was indeed a magnificent piece of nature. Scientists call it "Live Oak Tree" because it's evergreen almost. It does drop some leaves in the spring but quickly replaces them to keep the photosynthesis going. Mat and Alma were both good climbers and the big limbs of the tree were close to the ground, such that it was easy for them to climb them and even make few steps up and down like in a walk. They both knew lots of stories and liked to play the fictional characters, translating them into their reality. By turns, they were heroes fighting dragons, warriors conducing armies, fairies and elves with magical powers, and so on, about everything they knew from stories became alive around them.

"I'm Prince Matheo and you're Princess Alma, and this is our Castle. We lived together many hundreds of years ago, and we'll live together many more hundreds years from now."

"I wish I believe you."

"If you don't believe me, I'll find another princess, and I'll forget all about you."

"I don't want that. I better believe you and be your princess forever."

"Then we swear to be bond forever, for as long as we live. Would you?"

"Yes, and I believe you." They were only four and five years old, but they knew already the meaning of being bond to each other. Mat asked his father about the tree:

"How old could it be?"

"I would say between four hundred and five hundred years."

"How long it is going to live?"

"It looks strong and healthy, and it might have a time span of another five hundred years of life ahead."

In the coming year, Mat was enrolled in first grade of school and Alma in kindergarten.

Their schedule was different, and this time the

school bus took Mat from the gate and brought him back home. Nana kept driving Alma to kindergarten like before, waiting for her and bringing her back home.

"Don't you have anything to do around, instead of playing chauffeur to Alma?", Nora asked.

"I'm just helping Mya, Mrs. Doukas. She is very busy cooking for the crew, and I have time to spare. I asked permission from Dr. Doukas and he had no objection."

"I'm not surprised. He is always charitable."

When weather was good, Alma went to the gate, waiting for Mat to come from school. Holding hands, they walked on the country road going home, telling each other what they learned in that day and how much they missed each other. Mat was more knowledgeable than his classmates were, and many of the subjects taught by his teacher couldn't arouse his curiosity enough to give him pleasure.

"Maybe, next year you'll learn new things that you'll like and make you happy", Alma said, "I'll be in first grade, and I'll learn more than I know now, and I'll be happy."

"Yes, maybe you're right."

The school year finished and summer vacation was there. Mat and Alma could play again at their Castle and forget all about classes.

One day, Nora asked Philip:

"Would you like my family to come over and spend a little time with us?"

"Certainly. I'll be glad to meet your family and have it around. Invite the members of your family anytime you like, and make all the accommodations to feel them comfortable."

Nora called them and they were very pleased to spend some time on the farm, and especially meeting Mat. She told him that his two cousins will come over and be his guests, and she expected from him his best behavior. Mat was not at all pleased with that new perspective in his family, and told Alma about.

"We cannot see each other and play like now, because I'll have to entertain my two cousins and show them around. Whenever I can, I'll come to your house and see you. I hope they will not stay long."

"Are you going to show them our Castle?"

"Oh no! That place is sacred, is only yours and mine, and no one else is allowed to be there!"

After a week, the guests arrived, all in good spirits, and curious about that place, which only Jack knew about and saw it before.

Nora, Philip, and Mat were in front of the door, she made all the introductions and invited them inside.

"Everything is so beautiful!", Sarah said. "The air is so clean and one can see the blue sky, which we don't see very often."

Mat asked the girls, directly without any reserve:

"How old are you? Since you're twins, you must be of the same age. I'm seven."

"We're twelve", one of them answered.

"Let's go and I'll show you to your rooms", Nora said, "and after that we'll have lunch, since you must be hungry."

Betty outdid herself with the food she had prepared, more so that Nora would be pleased and have nothing to reproach.

"Everything is extremely tasty and well prepared. I wish I know how to cook some of these dishes", Sarah said.

"We're glad you like our food, and indeed, Betty is an excellent cook", Nora said.

The conversation was lingering awhile, everyone trying to find a common subject to talk about.

"Would you like to see the farm after lunch? I'll be glad to show you around if you're not tired and perhaps you'll prefer to take a nap first", Philip said.

"I don't know about Sarah and the girls, but I'm not tired and I'll be very pleased to see the farm", Jack said.

He didn't mention that he saw it even before Philip.

"We'll go too", everyone said.

"May I be excused?", Mat asked, "I have to check on Alma, she didn't feel well this morning."

"You can go", Philip said.

He called Joshua and asked him to join them and be the talking guide.

"By the way, Josh, how are Mya and Alma?"

"Very good, Philip, thank you."

After all the presentations he asked the family to follow him and gave it a tour of the farm for more than an hour. Sarah and the girls were very excited since they never have been on a farm, and everything was new for them. When back home, Joshua said:

"If you're not tired, I invite you this evening to a gathering of my people, around a bonfire, where you can listen to some Indian stories and some old songs."

Everyone approved with delight.

In the meantime, Mat went to Alma's room and found her reading a story on the computer. She was happy to see him:

"I missed you. I learned a new story and I'll tell you all about when we'll go to the Castle. How was your day?"

"I missed you a lot, and my day was a bore. My cousins are very nice, but they don't seem very bright. They are twelve years old and don't know much about the world around them. They talked between themselves and rarely addressed me or someone else. I think that they are very spoiled, since I understood that they can get everything they like from their parents."

"Don't be so harsh on them. Maybe they are shy, meeting you for the first time."

"Which side are you on?"

"Yours, but I was just saying. Are you coming tonight and join us around the bonfire?"

"I wouldn't miss it for the world. I must go now. See you tonight. Bye, my princess."

It was after seven o'clock evening when all joined the workers gathered around the bonfire. Philip saw Alma approaching and whispered to Mat in Greek:

"If ever I catch you lying again, you'll be in big trouble, young man."

"Sorry, Dad, I just wanted to get away and couldn't find another excuse."

"Next time, take me with you."

They both had an understanding, and a big smile. Together with the family they went to the Reids' house where close to it, the working people were already there, around the bonfire. They all sat on the ground, and Joshua gave them a short account of history in the Indian life.

"We all here, come from a long line of Indian tribes who first came about fifteen thousand years ago, possibly much earlier, from Asia, and from that time, a vast variety of cultures subsequently developed. More precisely, the native peoples from South Texas Plains are direct linear descendents of the *Paleoindian* peoples who came to the region about thirteen thousand years ago and whose descendents stayed on. Our most recent history dating from the 16th century is mentioned by the so-called *Coahuiltecan* cultures organized in small tribes derived from different sources tied to a common backing, and who first were hunter-gatherers. Our people of today, live in small villages around, preserve their heritage and work on the farms close by, to support their families. They are proud of their ancestry and they pass it on to every coming new generation. Now, let's enjoy some of the stories, which were well preserved and describe some of the significant historical times of our people."

One by one, the Indians narrated short stories about their heritage, about their native land, and about their families. The gathering ended with songs and dances around the bonfire. It was an extremely exciting and instructive evening for everyone. Only Philip knew the history of the Indian peoples.

In the next morning, Jack proposed a trip to town for doing some shopping.

"Anyone joining me?"

Everybody liked the idea, except for Mat and Philip; they chose to stay home. Jack approached Mat and said:

"Come with us, and I promise you'll enjoy this trip."

Mat looked at his father who said:

"Go Mat. We'll do some other time the planting in the greenhouse that we discussed earlier today."

On the way to Austin, they all talked about all kind of subjects, except Mat who kept silence. Jack asked him:

"What do you like to do most when you are not in school?"

"I like watching my father in the lab and learning about plants which he works on and making them stronger and healthier; he taught me lots of things that I wanted to know. I'll study the same branch of knowledge and become a scientist like him."

Everyone in the car kept silence and listened with wonder to Mat.

"This is a very commendable decision and I must say that I'm impressed", Jack said.

They arrived to downtown in Austin, parked the car and Jack said:

"You ladies go shopping everything you like and put it on my bill. Mat and I, will go find something interesting for men, and when you're ready, we'll meet in front of the bookstore and then we'll have lunch."

He took Mat by the hand and went to an electronics store. There were tens of brands, shapes, and sizes of microscopes on display. Jack talked to the seller, telling him what he wanted, and a knowledgeable vendor was called; he showed him a compound biological microscope kit with slides.

"This is yours, Mat, if you like it. Do you?"

Mat showed a big surprise on his face:

"This is a marvel, Uncle Jack, and I don't know what to say, except that I'm overwhelmed. Thank you kindly, but I cannot accept such a gift, which must be very expensive."

"If I couldn't afford to buy it, I wouldn't."

"Thank you again, but I rather would like not to have it, and in exchange, I would rather like you to buy a telescope for Alma. She loves gazing at the stars, and then she invents short stories, and writes about them; she is very intelligent. It will make her very happy and this will make me happy too."

Jack gave him a long look:

"You are very close to her, aren't you?"

"Yes, Uncle Jack, we are very close. When we'll grow up, she will become a writer and I'll be a scientist, but we'll be always together."

"I'll tell you what I think. I have no choice, but to buy a microscope for you and a telescope for Alma. How is that?"

"I never cry, Uncle Jack, but now I feel like I'm about to cry."

"Don't. You deserve my entire admiration, not only for your decision to become a scientist even if you're still so young, but also for your feelings and care you show for your friend."

He told the vendor what was their choice and

asked him to wrap up the microscope and the telescope.

Sarah called him on the cell phone:

"We're done. Where are you?"

"I'll call you when we're ready."

"Do you have a cell phone, Mat?"

"No."

"Then I have to buy one for you and one for Alma, such that you can be in touch when the weather outside is stormy and you cannot see each other. What do you say?"

"I think that I'm dreaming and I have to pinch myself to make sure that what is happening to me is real. I don't know how to thank you, because I cannot find the right words."

"No need for any words to thank me. I'm happy to have you as my nephew and this is my best reward. If you want anything else, just say it. I'm very rich, Mat, and I can afford everything you want from this store, no matter the cost."

"I don't want to impose Uncle Jack, but since you ask me, I would like very much to give Nana a cell phone so that she can talk to me anytime she wants. She raised me since I was born and she loves me dearly. Would this be an imposition, Uncle Jack?"

"Not a bit, Mat. Let's have a cell phone for Nana also."

He asked the vendor to activate all three cell

phones, register them to his name, and make sure that the bills will be send to his address in Midland.

"I only can say thank you for everything you did for me, Uncle Jack. I'll never forget you and this day, when you made me so happy."

"I'll never forget you, Mat, and this day when you made me so happy, also."

They met the ladies in front of the bookstore, loaded the car with the many packages with whatever they bought, and went to the restaurant to have lunch. It was late afternoon when they started the trip back to the farm.

Once there, everybody was excited about the good time spent in town, unwrapped the packages, and showed each other the purchases they had made. Sarah bought a nice dress for Alma, and Nora bought a wristwatch for Philip and one for Mat, who expressed his gratitude politely and with a kind smile. Nana received her cell phone with great pleasure, saying that now she will be able to keep track of Mat. Philip was in his lab, and Mat rushed over and called him to join the others. He was very pleased with the present given to him by Nora, and very impressed by the gifts Jack bought for Mat.

"This is awesome, Jack. Thank you kindly, but it's a bit complicated for his age."

"Mat will learn fast how to use it. He already chose his career and told me that he wants to be a scientist like his father."

"He has enough time to decide. I don't necessarily encourage him to become a scientist, but I try to develop his curiosity in learning and acquiring knowledge in every field he likes. Thank you again, Jack, and maybe we should go to the lab and see how we can install this marvelous instrument."

They went there, Philip made space on a small table next to his, and in very short time, he installed the microscope for Mat. Just to check how it works he looked at some slides and said:

"This is better than expected. Everything is clear to the finest details. Mat, you have a scientific jewelry here; make sure that you use it wisely, to each level of knowledge. We'll go slowly, step by step, such that you'll be able to understand and work on the miracle of life in plants."

"I promise never to disappoint you, Dad."

"This is good enough for me, my dearest."

"Can you spare some time now and go with me to Alma's house and install the telescope Uncle Jack bought for her?"

"Let's go."

Everyone wanted to be there and watch how Alma will take the news. They went to her house, Joshua and the crew just came from the field, and Mya was ready to serve dinner. Alma opened the door and was surprised by all those people coming over at that late hour.

"Yes?", she only could ask.

"Let's go inside, Alma", Mat said, "we have something for you."

Joshua and Mya showed up and were no less surprised than their daughter was.

Just to speed up the meeting, Philip said:

"My relatives here, bought some presents for Alma, and we all came to see her for that purpose. May we come in?"

They went inside, Sarah gave her the nice dress, and Alma got excited. She tried to find the right words to thank her, but she only could say:

"Thank you kindly Mrs. Wilson. It's very beautiful and I'm going to wear it only for special occasions. You're very kind to me."

"You're welcome, Alma. You're a very pretty girl and very well educated. I'm very pleased that I've met you."

"Now let's see the other present, and for this we have to step out on the balcony", Philip said.

They unpacked the telescope and when Alma saw it, she let out a scream of wonder mixed with joy.

"Is this for me?", she shouted so loud that probably people outside the farm could hear her.

"Yes, Alma, this is all yours, and my uncle Jack bought it for you, when he bought for me a microscope."

The little girl started crying and words of thanks came mixed with her tears. Even Mat who knew her well, was very touched by her feelings. He took her hand and said:

"Don't cry like a little girl. Just say thanks to my uncle and behave yourself."

Alma always listened to him. She composed herself and said:

"Thank you Uncle Jack, from the bottom of my heart."

"Your heart is big Alma, as your kindness, and as your soul. Use it for gazing at the stars, make up stories, and write them all. One day, you'll be a famous writer, and maybe we'll both remember this evening."

He came close to her and embraced her with warmth.

Philip installed the telescope and by turn, after Alma, everyone looked at the stars that had already begun their parade in the August sky. Mat came close to his little friend and gave her the cell phone:

"This is for you also. I have one too. Uncle Jack said that we can be in touch when the weather outside is stormy and we cannot see each other. I know your number and now write down my number. I'll call you when I get home."

Other thanks and other expression of joy followed, impressing everyone around watching those two children who cared so much for each other. Ever since, Alma took up in earnest her study about cosmos, by reading books for her age, using her telescope, and taking notes about the stars.

Time went by, Mat was twelve years old, and Alma eleven. They both learned a lot in the past years, and as before, shared their knowledge, exchanging opinions and making plans for the future. They usually met at their Castle, but not playing anymore, fairies, elves, and warriors. They sat on their favorite branches and talked a lot. Alma showed him the stories she wrote lately and Mat was always there to give her suggestions and express his opinions. One day, Alma couldn't be more surprised when she read on the trunk of the tree: *This is the Castle of Prince Matheo and Princess Alma who lived here happily ever after.*

"I carved this inscription on your favorite branch, and will be there for as long as we'll live."

She caressed his beautiful face:

"We'll be together for as long as we'll live."

At home, each one followed their daily schedule, doing their school assignments, and after that, reading a lot about what they were interested. Mat also, spent time in the lab, next to his father who showed him every step of the experiment he worked on. One day, Nora told Philip:

"We don't need the nanny anymore, and we should let her go. Mat is now old enough to take care of himself and he doesn't need a babysitter at his age. I think it will be better for him to go to a boarding school where he can get a good education and a good discipline."

"Over my dead body. Or yours! The nanny will stay exactly where she is. If you remember correctly, she raised Mat since he was born, because he didn't have a mother. She will continue to take care of Mat, as she did before, no matter what age is he now or tomorrow, or the day after."

"As you wish, but I think she became useless."

"You are not in the position to make a judgment in this matter. End of discussion."

A few more years went by. Mat was sixteen years old and Alma was fifteen. They started kissing and experienced new feelings for each other. It was time for puberty to talk about. Philip asked both to come over to his lab and he called Mya. He gave them a thorough lesson about their age and what they are supposed to do and to expect. Mya explained also many aspects encountered at their age and made some comments to Philip's lecture. Both, Mat and Alma understood very well and learned in that day many things that were unknown to them.

A new kind of love grew between them. One day, Mat went to Alma's house. Her room was still keeping the ambience of a little girl from years before. They kissed and embraced each other with all the love, which sprung with new mysterious meanings, unrevealed until then. The boy and girl became man and woman with one body and one soul.

In fall, Mat enrolled in college at Austin University, and Alma entered the last grade of high school. They couldn't see each other because Mat lived on campus and came home only for vacation. Only on the phone they could talk and share they feelings and thoughts with love and same care for each other.

In the beginning of the following summer, Alma graduated with honor, and Mat came home for vacation. She applied for college at the University of Texas at San Antonio, since it was closer to her home. Mat grew tall, had a strong body, and resembled his father more than anyone could say. He looked like a younger brother to Philip, rather than like his son. Alma grew too, she was slim, taller than average height, and very pretty. Her narrow, hooded eyes showing warmth all the way up to piercing glance, always looked straight at people. The dark green color of her eyes, and her golden, wavy, blond hair complimented each other in a harmonious combination.

In the middle of summer, Joshua died of heart attack. Mya and Alma were devastated. Philip and Nana felt like losing the best friend they ever trusted and was close to them. Nora waited only a few days after funerals, to show her feelings:

"Mya and Alma have to go and vacate their dwelling", she said to Philip.

"Don't you have any heart left and any compassion? Where are they supposed to go after sixteen years of living on the farm and becoming like family to us?"

"Your family, not mine. I've already found a foreman who will manage the farm; he will move in, after two weeks. I'll give them notice and they have to comply with my decision."

She called Mya and told her to leave in two weeks.:

"Take only your personal belongings and nothing else. Good luck!"

"You need more luck than me. I have my work and I'll survive."

Mya talked with Alma, trying both to find the right choice for their uncertain future. They both came to the conclusion that San Antonio was the best place for them to settle down and have a home in that town. Nana found out about Nora's decision and rushed to their place:

"I'm coming with you. I have money saved over the years, and I can help to make a living for us three. Mat is in college most of the year, and I don't feel being all the time in Nora's way."

Mya and Alma embraced her and were very pleased with her decision.

"We chose San Antonio for a place to settle down. Austin would have been better, but Nora has an apartment there, where she goes often.

It might happen that we meet each other on the street or in a shop, and I don't want that."

"Good thinking Mya. What will be the first step?"

"Tomorrow, Alma and I, we'll go out there to find a place for the three of us, where we can live, and from there, we'll see what to do. I also have a bit of money saved over the years, and maybe later I'll buy a bakery. For now, I'll be looking for a job, and Alma will prepare for college."

Next day, Mya and Alma drove to San Antonio and took them less than two hours to get there. The town was crowded, people were shopping, walking, having a coffee outside diner places, or kept busy driving from place to place. They parked the car, enter a coffee shop, took a seat, and Alma bought a map of the town and a newspaper looking for an apartment. They needed something close to downtown where one of the university campus was located, most of the stores were open until late night, and buses came from all directions. She found a two-bedroom apartment, with living room, one bathroom, and kitchen, not far from where they were. On their way to that place, Mya said:

"You'll have your room and I'll share the other one with Nana. I think this will be a comfortable dwelling for us."

The apartment was on the corner of the building, it was clean, with big windows, and had a small balcony; Mya paid the security deposit and first month rent.

"We'll go shopping for furniture and household needs, when we'll move in. Now, let's have lunch and go back to the farm."

Nana waited for them with impatience; she was very pleased with what they did.

"We'll leave ten days from now", Mya said. "We'll take my pickup truck and you can leave your car here. It's old anyway, and we can buy you a new one over there."

Meantime, Mat and Alma made plans to see each other when they both will be away. From San Antonio to Austin was a drive for about one hour and a half covering eighty miles, which could be easily done over the weekends by either of them. Until then, in those ten days left, they met at their Castle, and had long talks about everything became dear to them in those sixteen years of their young lives. Alma acquired a lot of knowledge about the universe, stars and planets, and she liked to share it with Mat:

"You know what is most important from what I've learned? If the planets in our solar system would have been closer or farther from the sun, life could not have existed on our planet. This means that they did not appear by chance, but were created for a specific purpose. What that purpose might be, nobody knows and probably nobody will ever know."

"What you're saying is true, since a same purpose applies to the evolution of life on Earth. Life started eons ago as one bacterium in a drop of water and evolved into the world we know today. The human mind is a miracle that couldn't appear by chance; it evolved from simple exposure to the needs for survival until the brilliant revelations of science, art, philosophy, and technology of our today's world. The universe and the human evolution must be linked together by a common goal because their development was initiated and continued with the precision of the laws that guide the atom and subatomic particles. What that goal is for, nobody could ever know, but the only logic explanation for me, is that nothing happened by chance, and there is a Creator of the universe, of life, and of the human mind."

Both were on their way up to become prince and princess of the intellectual elite.

In the last day, they took pictures of each other with their Castle in the background, as a reminder of the most treasured place they knew.

Time for leaving was there; Mat and Philip came to the pickup truck, and helped Mya and Nana to load their belongings; Philip gave them outstanding references in case they'll need them for a job. They embraced each other and promised to stay in touch. Mya and Nana cried, while Alma and Mat felt like numb. Philip had tears in his eyes and didn't bother to wipe them away when they flowed down his cheeks.

Mat and Philip waited on top of the road, until the pickup truck disappeared from their view.

The path of life was again into the wind, for those people who built trust, care, and love among them, over the many years of knowing each other, and hoping that the bond between them will stand the test of a long time.

Chapter 2

Gusty Wind

Returned to the house, Philip went to his lab, trying to restore his feelings and put together his thoughts. Mat went to Nana's room, sat on her bed, held tightly her pillow, and sobbed with convulsive gasps like never before. Suddenly a fit of rage seized him; he sprang up and ran all over the house to find Nora; she was in her study reading some papers. Mat opened the door by hitting it against the wall and started yelling at her:

"What did you do?! You took from me my only mother I had and cherished! You took from me the love of my life! You took from me my trustworthy and dear friend! You took them all and threw them on the street! What kind of monster are you?"

Nora was stunned. She dropped the paper she was handling and only said:

"Watch your tongue, boy."

"I'm not your boy, you dirty garbage, what you are!"

Philip heard him yelling so loud that the entire house resounded. He left his work and rushed to the scene, when Mat was about to strike Nora with his fist.

"You are nothing but a miserable, despicable, low life creature that doesn't deserve to live! I hope you rot in hell!"

Philip was behind him right in time to catch his arm before Mat could strike her. He took him by the shoulder and only said:

"Don't do it. Let's go, my son."

Mat was shivering and gasping for air; Philip took him to his room and tried to calm him down, without any success.

"How could you marry such a monster?"

"She was not like that when we met; she was a warm, loving, and caring person; she changed a lot over the years. Let's try together to find our calm so that we can reason correctly. We'll talk about this tomorrow. Now it's late and we both need some sleep."

It never occurred to Philip that his attitude toward Nora made a major contribution to the changes she was going through. From the very beginning of their marriage, Philip was deeply concerned only with his work and research, completely neglecting his relationship with Nora. She was left alone most of the time and it was an appropriate reaction for her to look for connections with people outside the family, seeking for what she needed the most and missed badly: warmth and understanding. When she gave birth to her baby, Nora assumed it was a threat meant to destroy her husband's feelings of warmth and love for her. The pressure and insecurity increased in her soul, as did the distance from Philip. If he had had an attitude of closeness to her, if he had had a sense of attention and warmth, Nora would not have been so refractory to her own child; she would have accepted him and loved him. Her character would not have been so stubborn against a difficult situation that she could no longer control and which led to an increased tension between them. Philip did not try to understand the crisis she was going through and which was caused by the constant neglect he always had towards her. The distance between them increased and completely distorted the relationships that should have been normal in a marriage. If Philip had behaved like a caring and loving husband, Nora would have had a proper attitude of a wife and mother who would have loved her family. Instead, she changed drastically for worse.

In that evening, Philip put Mat to bed, and gave him a strong sedative.

"Don't go, Dad. Stay with me and hold me."

"I'll be next to you, and I'll hold you all night."

In few minutes, he was asleep, and Philip lay

down next to him, holding him in his arms. Late evening, Alma called, and Philip answered the phone:

"Mat is asleep, Alma. He took hard your departure, and I gave him a sedative. How are you doing?"

"We are all right, Uncle Philip. We have a nice apartment, bought everything we needed, and now we try to adjust as much as we can. Is Mat all right, Uncle Philip, or you're trying to hide something from me?"

"He is fine, Alma, only exhausted by the events of the day. He'll call you in the morning. Give my love to Nana and Mya. Good night my dear."

"We miss you Uncle Philip. Good night."

The next morning, both felt rested and in a better shape.

"Let's go out to Tilden, have breakfast and after that, a refreshing walk in the park and a father-to-son, nice talk", Philip said.

First, Mat called Alma:

"How are you my love? Dad said that you called last night, but I was asleep. I'm sorry I've missed your call."

"Are you all right? I miss you so that I have no words to say. Maybe one of these days you and Uncle Philip will come to see us."

"It's a promise. How is my Nana and Auntie Mya?"

"Good. They both are busy with our new household."

"Give them a big hug and a kiss. I love you my dearest. I'm going now with Dad, to Tilden for breakfast and a walk in the park, just to get away from this place. I'll see you soon."

"Give a kiss to Uncle Philip. Bye dearest. I love you too."

Mat hesitated a bit before asking:

"Dad, when can I access my trust fund account?"

"I told you before, when you'll be twenty-one".

"What if I need money sooner?"

"You have your allowance."

"Dad, could you do me a favor?"

"Just say it."

"I would like very much to buy for Alma a gold heart shaped locket, opening two sides, where to insert her picture and mine. I have some money saved from my allowance, but I don't think it's enough. Can you help?"

"Of course, I can. Let's go."

It took them only minutes to drive those ten miles from the farm. They first had a hearty breakfast to satiate their appetite since they didn't eat anything the day before. After that, they went to a reputable jewelry store. The jeweler put in front of them a rich assortment of pendants. Mat chose a heart shaped one with a small emerald on top.

"It's her birthday stone, Dad", Mat said.

When he heard the price, he became silent, and then said in Greek:

"This is too expensive. We cannot afford it. Let's see another one."

"We'll take it", Philip said in Greek also. "I like this one too, and we can manage about the price, don't worry."

"I don't know what to say, Dad, except that I'm awfully happy."

"That's good enough for me."

"Would you like an inscription on back?", the jeweler asked.

"Everlasting love", Mat answered, "and also, I would like you to cut and insert these two pictures."

He took from his wallet the pictures made in the last day of their meeting at the Castle.

"I'll be glad to do that; I'll be back in few minutes. Have a seat."

The jeweler went to his lab and returned after less than half hour. Mat and Philip were overjoyed when they saw the locket. They also bought a white gold bracelet for Nana and one for Mya.

"You spent a lot of money, Dad."

"I'm not broke, yet. Let's go have lunch first and then we go to the park for a walk."

It was the end of the week and people took time for shopping, walking, and having good time. The park was all green in that day of August, children played around, while parents sat on benches, talking and watching them.

"Do you think that I might have inherited Nora's genes of becoming as bad as she is?"

"No, Mat. She doesn't have genes of violence or of a serial killer. Her parents were honest, good, and hard working people. They passed on their genetics to their children and nothing bad came out of this. Nora chose to be the way she is. She is selfish, arrogant, has not a bit of consideration for anyone, and she thinks only about what is good for her. She doesn't care if she hurts people or if people like her or not. Money, excitement, relations with rich and famous stimulate her feelings to behave the way she does. Her reactions to conduct herself toward others, or taking bad decisions, are only determined by the behavior she chooses, based on her character. Behavioral traits are not inherited; they are acquired and shaped over time by everyone's choices. As you can see, there is nothing for you to worry about becoming like her."

"I'm completely relieved, Dad. I was thinking a lot lately and I became not only worried, but also frightened. Now I feel much, much better."

"I'm glad I could answer correctly to your question. You know what I'll like us to do? I would very much like us to drive tomorrow to San Antonio and see our adoptive family. What do you think?"

"I'm thrilled, because I wanted the same thing, but I thought that it might be too early, since they just got there and maybe they are busy to adjust their pace with their new surroundings."

"Only one way to find out. We'll go, and maybe we can help with their arrangement."

They returned home and found out from Irene that Nora left for Austin and didn't say when she will be back.

Next morning they woke up in a joyful spirit and started their trip to San Antonio. On the way, Philip asked:

"We still have one full month vacation until the school starts. Would you like to do some research in the lab, on your own? I know you're very young, but most scientists started their first experiments as teenagers."

"I can try, if you explain me the procedure I have to follow."

"I think you've learned quite a bit until now to be able to do the experiment. I like you to do some hybridization, which as you know, is a crossing of genes originated in different species; this is an old procedure, known for long time. What I want you to experiment, is to find the most useful gene of one plant or the other to become predominant, and be transferred to the offspring. In this way, the resulting plant will grow stronger, larger, and healthier than its parents. I wrote a paper on this subject long ago and I was awarded. Some of the plants grown on my section of the farm resulted from similar experiments, which I conducted first in the greenhouse. This will be a good exercise for you if you want to go farther and learn about plants at the molecular level. In the meantime, I'll work on my project and be next to you, anytime you'll need my attention. What do you say?"

"I'm enthusiastic, Dad. I'll be proud of myself if I'll be able to perform with success this experiment."

"I agree, and I'm already proud of you."

After little more than one hour, they arrived in town, and started looking for the address. At the corner of the street, was a six-story building and the family lived at the second floor. Alma opened the door, and without any words, she jumped into Mat's arms kissing him lovingly. In a minute, Nana showed up, started crying, and embraced them both.

"Mya is in town looking for a job", she said. The owner of a bakery, not far from here, promised her the position of kitchen help, if someone who applied before will not be available. She will be home soon."

Shortly after, Mya was there. They embraced each other with warmth, and she said:

"I got the job, and I'll start tomorrow! I'll be helping the owner's wife in the kitchen, cleaning, dish washing, and assist her in the production of baking; it's not much paid, it's tough work, but it's a good start for me. Now, tell me about you two, how have you been since we've seen each other?"

"First, we missed you", Philip said, "and we

didn't do much, except that we both worked in the lab, and this was a good time to spend."

"We have something for you and Nana", Mat said.

He gave them the bracelets, which came as a big surprise for both, and gave them a great pleasure.

"I need a few private moments to talk to Alma", he said, "it won't take long."

"Let's go to the other room", Alma said.

Nobody knew what they said to each other, but shortly after they came out with tears in their eyes.

"Look Mom and Nana, what Mat gave me!"

She showed them the locket which was indeed beautiful, displaying charm and elegance on her pale skin.

"This is awesome, and I've never seen something like this", Mya said, and she was joined by Nana:

"I'm getting emotional and feel like crying. You two indeed love each other more than I could expect, and I'm happy for you both. Now, let's have lunch, since you must be hungry. Give me a few moments, and I'll prepare something."

"We'll go and eat out, if you know a good place around or even farther", Philip said.

They went out, walking to a small diner, which was close to the bakery where Mya was hired.

"Here is the place where I'll be working," she said when they came by.

The bakery was located on the ground floor of a building with ten floors, where Mya said, the apartments were so expensive to rent that only rich people could afford. The diner was next to the bakery, and quite crowded at that hour; the owner showed them a table close to the window, handed them the menu, suggesting the best choice.

After lunch, they took a walk along the line of boutiques and stores, until they arrived in front of one of the three university campuses. It was huge and impressive.

"I'll be learning here, on this campus", Alma said, "I've already applied for college when I graduated from high school, and I was accepted. I'll take classes in English Literature and Writing because I want to become a writer and maybe a teacher. Also, I'll continue to learn more about Astronomy, since this is one of my passions, and maybe one day I'll write a real story about stars. In the same time, I'll look for a part-time job, and I would like very much to work in the campus library. Maybe, I'll find an opening there."

"I'm very impressed, Alma", Philip said "and I must congratulate you for the splendid career you chose. You figured out to details everything you want to do and to expect. I'm very proud of you."

"Thank you, Uncle Philip; since I was a little girl I wanted to become a writer. It's a feeling I have that this will be my right choice to make something good of myself."

He embraced her with warmth:

"You'll be a great writer and probably very famous. I can't wait to watch your success."

They visited the library, which was amazingly well organized with the usually different sections easy to find and check the subjects. It was the best place to do research and write academic papers.

"Here I would like to work. Tomorrow morning I'll come and talk to the Director of Library and ask for an entry-level job, considering that I have no experience", Alma said.

"I'll tell you what you can ask for and you don't need experience but only high school", Philip said. "There is a position in every academic library which is called *Library Aide Reference Assistant,* and is supervised by the Library Assistant. The job consists of overall daily maintenance of the library, to include ordering, cataloging, classifying, and some customer service to library patrons. If they have here an opening, take it and you'll learn a lot."

"I don't know how to thank you Uncle Philip. I never knew that such position exists."

"Make sure that you answer truthfully and correct to all the questions when you'll be interviewed. Don't try to hide anything and don't try to flourish the answers. Keep it simple and correct, and you'll get the job. I can go with you, I'm very well known at this university, but rather I'd like you to get it on your own without using my influence and protection."

"I like it better this way, too, Uncle Philip."

It was late afternoon when they returned to the apartment. Philip and Mat were ready to go home when Nana asked:

"Can't you stay a few days more? We don't know when we'll see each other again. We can accommodate you for the night, it might not be very comfortable, but we can manage."

They both looked at each other in agreement, and Philip said:

"It's vacation time and we can spare a few more pleasant days to be with you. Nevertheless, we'll go to a hotel and have a room there, and we'll be all more comfortable. Where is the nearest hotel?"

"Not far from the campus", Mya said.

She gave them directions to follow, and added:

"Tomorrow I'll start my job, and Alma has to go for the interview, but we'll see you later."

"We'll come over in the morning, and we'll drive Alma to the campus, and wait for her in the cafeteria. Nana can come with us. What do you say?"

"I love this", Alma said, and Nana approved:

"Me too, and so she will not feel scared if she will know that we are close by."

Philip and Mat went to the hotel, and had a good night sleep until late morning. Before ten o'clock they went to pick up Alma and Nana, and drove to the campus. The interview lasted for about one hour. Alma was pleased the way it came out and said:

"It wasn't that hard, and the Director of Library, was very nice, showed interest in the presentation I made about my background and about being already enrolled in this college. He said that one more applicant has to come for an interview, and he will make his decision by the end of the week. I'm confident because I know I can do the job, the way he described it."

They all embraced her, wishing her to be optimistic, no matter what the outcome will be.

"I read in the paper that the children hospital is looking for qualified nurses", Nana said, "and I'm very tempted to try for this job. What do you think?"

"What are you waiting for? Where is the hospital? Let's go there and find out", Philip said.

"It's quite far from here, but I know the address."

It took them about an hour to get there. Nana went to the personnel administration while the three others waited in the hall. After more than two hours, she showed up, smiling and gesturing quickly:

"I got the job! The Manager of Human Resources, asked me a thousand questions and was pleased with my background. The letter of reference you gave me, Philip, helped a lot, and he read it several times. I can start next Monday, and be there at eight o'clock. I have to wake up early, since I need to take two buses to get there, but this doesn't bother me at all. I'm awfully happy! I would like to call Mya, but she is not supposed to be disturbed. I'll tell her tonight."

"You are one of a kind, Nana! Everyone will love you there, especially the children. We love you, too, a lot!", Alma said.

Mat kissed her on her cheeks, and Philip embraced her with warmth. It was already past three o'clock and they were famished, since none of them had breakfast; they had lunch and went to the apartment waiting for Mya. She came around five and looked tired but felt very happy listening to the good news happened in that day. Late evening, Philip and Mat went to the hotel and had a long chat before going to bed.

The next morning, after breakfast, they went to the apartment; Mya was long gone to work, and Philip said:

"I'll have to do some shopping today and I suggest that Nana comes with me. You two, have some good time, doing what you like and we'll meet later. Give us a call if you feel like joining us for lunch. Bye, now."

Nana and Philip left, and on the way out, she asked:

"You think that it's wise to leave them alone?"

"This is exactly why I intended to do, Nana. They both are almost grown-ups, they adore each other, and they need to spend time in privacy."

"If you say so, but I'm worried."

"Don't be. Come, let's go shopping something I need for my lab, and then we'll go find something nice for you."

It was around two o'clock when Alma called Nana:

"We're hungry and want to meet you for lunch. We'll come over to the diner in few minutes."

They showed up, said that they talked a lot in that morning about their future, and felt like the bond between them becomes stronger with every passing day. Mat whispered to Philip:

"Thank you."

His father only nodded and caressed his head. In that evening, they said that they will leave in the next day and took farewell from each other, making lots of promises.

On the way home, Philip said:

"I never expected everything coming so well for them. They have a good place to stay, good jobs, they are healthy, and most of all they are our beloved family."

"I'm happy for them, Dad, and I'm happy for us, too. There is no better family than you and I could have."

Nana managed to buy a used car and tried it on her way to work, but gave up after a couple of days. Because of the heavy traffic, she chose to ride the bus, even if it took longer to get in time.

Meanwhile, Nora went to Austin and threw party after party in her apartment, inviting her rich friends and her former companion who was always there for her and who was well paid for his services. She just needed to go away from the farm and try to forget that horrible scene between her and Mat. Thinking about that day, she needed to take a decision and act somehow to improve the climate in her house. She thought over and over, and decided to have a talk with Mat and defending her attitude. After all, he was her son, no matter how far they were one from the other. She went home and arrived one day before them. Betty told her that they left last week and didn't say where they were going or when they'll be back.

Philip and Mat arrived home and went directly to the lab, both feeling the gloomy atmosphere surrounding them.

"We still have about three weeks vacation and we'll work on the project we talked about", Philip said, "and after that, you go to campus and I'll stay in town, and we can see each other every day in school."

The door opened and Nora showed up:

"Where have you been?"

"Out", Philip answered.

"I asked where?"

"And I said out."

She turned around and left. Her good intentions to improve the climate went down the drain, but she was not ready to give up her plan.

After a couple of days, Nora went to Mat's

room and knocked at the door. He didn't answer, knowing that his father was in the greenhouse planting the newly developed seeds. Mat just came to his room to pick up some slides and was ready to leave and join his father. Nora entered the room and said:

"Could I have a word with you, if you don't mind?"

"I do mind, and I'm busy. What do you want?"

"I was thinking lately about the way I behaved, and I regret how I treated those people, but I had to replace the foreman as soon as possible. I couldn't keep them here, since I couldn't provide any jobs for them. I hope you understand."

"I understand. Anything else?"

"I wish you and I could have a fresh start and a better relationship. What do you say?"

"If you won't be in my way, and I'll be not in your way, and if we don't see each other, but only occasionally, I would say that this will be a new start and a better relationship. Now I have to go to the lab and work with my father."

He left, and Nora was completely disappointed. She hoped that Mat will forgive her and give her another chance for reconciliation. Nevertheless, she was determined not to give in to her plan and intended to reorganize her strategy. For the time being, she had to get out of that atmosphere and went to Austin, just to forget about everything, postponing her strategy and plans. Other parties with her friends helped her to relax and have a good time.

One morning, James came to see Philip and asked to have a word with him:

"You are my mentor and my best friend", he said, "but I have to tell you this, because I don't want you to get hurt. Nora is not behaving the way she should when she comes to town. I saw her twice kissing with a man on the street and it wasn't the same man. What are you going to do?"

"Nothing. Thank you for telling me. Nora sees life and marriage in a different way than I see them. When the time comes, I'll talk to her, but not now."

In the following days, Philip and Mat worked on the project with good results that still had to be experimented in the field. By the end of the week, Alma called and told them that she got the job, and she will start Monday, working about eighteen hours a week. Both Mat and Philip were overjoyed.

Fall was already there with the beginning of the school year. One day, James came to Philip's office and said:

"I'm getting married next week, and I'll be honored if you and Mat will come to my wedding."

"I wouldn't miss it for the world. Who is the lucky bride?"

"Her name is Vera Thompson and she works in the lab. She is very bright, very kind, and very charming. We are about the same age and we share a lot of feelings and knowledge."

"Congratulations to you both. Mat and I will be happy to attend your wedding and meet your bride."

The next Sunday, Philip and Mat went to the church, attended the marriage ceremony, and after that, they went to the banquet hall at the restaurant. The families of the groom and bride seated on the podium while all the guests were invited to sit at the round tables. Mat sat next to Philip who had his place next to a pleasant woman. The atmosphere was enjoyable, and speeches followed one after another. Everyone seemed to have a great time, talking loud to each other, even if they didn't show something special to say. Philip exchanged a few words with the woman next to him, and noticed that she had a very smooth and warm voice and a charming smile. They introduced to each other only by names and not specifying anything else. After dinner was served, James and his bride toured the tables and thanked everyone for coming. Approaching Philip, he said:

"Please meet my bride, Philip. This is Vera, and we both thank you and Mat for coming. I can see that you are sitting next to my favorite lady in my family. In case you haven't been introduced, this is my aunt Samantha Harris, and she is member of the faculty, professor of Philosophy. Aunt Sam, this is my mentor and my friend, Doctor Philip

Doukas, professor of Biotechnology at graduate school. This is his son, Mat, he is in first year of college, and we know each other since he was born. Please enjoy the rest of the evening, and thank you again for coming."

Mat stood up, went around Philip's chair, and kissed with grace her hand:

"I'm very pleased Professor Harris to meet you."

"Likewise, Mat. You look very much like your father."

"Thank you. That's what everyone says."

The music started, inviting the guests on the dance floor.

"I wish, Alma were here", Mat said, "she knows how to dance, and I don't."

"I can teach you, Mat," Samantha said.

"No, I'll be your partner for the evening", Philip said. "I'll tell you, Mat what you can do. See that elderly lady, over there? She looks like she needs a partner. I'm sure she can teach you how to dance, and in the meantime, considering her age, you'll not feel unfaithful to Alma. What do you think?"

"I'll go and try."

Mat invited her to dance telling her from the beginning that he doesn't know even the simple steps. The lady was very flattered to be asked to dance with him. It seemed that Mat enjoyed that experience, since he danced all evening without a pause. Meantime, Philip danced with Samantha, talking and having short laughs in the same time, until the evening was over. When time to part, Philip said:

"I'll give you a call, Sam."

"I can't wait, Philip."

On their way out, Mat said:

"Are you in love with her?"

"No, but I might be. She is very pleasant, very intelligent, and we have lot of knowledge that we can share and talk about."

"I wish you'll be in love with her and for a change have a wonderful life with a normal woman."

"I wish that too, and I'll let you know if such a miracle will happen. I'll take you now to your room and I'll go to mine. We'll see each other in school. Sleep well, my son."

"Good night, Dad, and I must say that I had a wonderful time with that lady. I know how to dance now, but I have to tell Alma how I've learned. She will be amused."

Philip and Sam started dating, and in short time, they fell in love. He was forty-eight years old, and she was forty-five, both at the age when love becomes the richness valued by a disciplined mind. She was married long ago, but the marriage didn't work out. He told her about his life and his rocky marriage, being not able to divorce Nora, who'll never let him go mostly because she liked to attend his lectures outside the school and tell everyone that she was his wife. He also told her that he has a big project in progress on the farm started years ago, and if he would ask Nora for a divorce, she will destroy it without giving him the divorce.

"Can you take me the way I am?"

"I'll take you any way you are. I love you and this is all that's matters. We have to be cautious, meet only at late hours, never go dining out, or shopping together. She will never find out about us."

Indeed, Nora never did.

Meanwhile, the family in San Antonio adjusted quite well to the new climate in which they had to live. They all had jobs and only little time to see each other, mostly in the evening. Mya was on her feet all day long, but she liked her job and was much appreciated by the owners. Nana had to take care mostly of children with acute and chronic infectious diseases under direct supervision of the pediatric specialist. She had a lot of responsibility as a nurse, but she also spent time with the ill children, talking to them and trying to make them feel comfortable. Alma learned quickly her job as aide assistant, which mainly consisted in sorting material according to classification or catalogue numbers and returning library materials to shelves or other storage areas. Most of the time she worked with computers and proved to be more knowledgeable than expected.

After work, the three of them met at home, and

found a great pleasure to talk about their busy day. Mat came to visit over the weekend, spending a wonderful time together, and having long chats in private with Alma. He told them about his father having a relationship with Sam and how marvelous they both were.

"I took her class and she is an amazing teacher", Mat said.

"Why? Did you want to check on her, or did you want to become smarter?", Alma asked.

"Both, and I must say that she is very special and I like her a lot. I think she likes me too."

Mat came often to see them, but only on weekends when he had no school. From Austin to San Antonio was a drive for about one hour and a half and that was easy for him to do.

One evening, Alma told her mother and Nana, that she wanted to apply for a room on campus, since she worked in the library and the classes were in the next building. Her scholarship will pay, and it will be left enough for food and her other expenses. They both agreed, mostly because in that way she could save time and avoid stress. Even if it was a little late, Alma applied for a room and her part-time job in the library helped a lot to get it.

Shortly after, she got the room, it was small but cozy and comfortable. Mya and Nana helped her to move out and arrange her belongings in her new habitation.

"You did this because you wanted to have privacy with Mat", Mya said.

"This was only part of the reason. If my mother wouldn't understand me, who else would?"

"Yes, I understand you, just be careful."

"I will, don't worry, and thank you for everything."

Alma called Mat and told him the news; he was overjoyed. In the coming weekend, he came over, and when she opened the door, he didn't say a word, but kissed her with passion.

The next day he had to leave and told her that the following weekend he might not come because he had to go to the farm and finish a project.

Mat told his father all about when they both were in the lab on the farm.

"I'm so happy, I can't even tell you", Philip said.

Nora was close to the door and heard him.

"Why are you so happy about?", she asked.

"Mat wrote a paper in school and got the highest grade", he answered.

"Oh, that? I thought it was something more exciting. Listen, Philip, I wanted to talk with you about what I would like to do. I was thinking to add more rooms to the house and making bigger, what do you think?"

"Why? Do you need more rooms to give bigger parties? I thought you do this in town and not here on the farm."

"Not for parties. I was thinking that Mat will

get married one day and have children, and so the house will be bigger and more pleasant."

"Maybe he won't live on the farm, and so you don't have to worry about him getting married and having children. You don't even like children. You only like living in town, throwing big parties, and kissing men on the street."

"Who told you that?"

"Someone who saw you."

"What? She kissed men on the street?", Mat asked and he burst out laughing. "I assume that the rest of the procedure was performed in a dark alley!", and he continued laughing.

"Those were old acquaintances and not flirtations or love affairs", Nora tried to defend herself.

"I didn't ask who they were, because I don't give a damn on what you're doing. Just don't tell everyone that you're 'Mrs. Doukas', and try to be more discreet."

Nora felt like a slap on her face; she lost and Philip won the battle with a high score. She opened her mouth to say something, but Philip turned around and said:

"Let's go Mat, we'll be late for the conference."

While in the car, he said:

"Let's go take Sam, and we'll all go to see the family and Alma's new home. We had work to do today, but I don't feel like being on the farm after that conversation with Nora. What do you say?"

"I couldn't agree more. Let's go."

Sam was enthusiastic about the trip:

"I have some papers to work on, but they don't go anywhere and can wait."

Mat called Alma and told her that the three of them were on their way to town.

"Mom and Nana will be late from work, and you have to come directly to my room. I can't wait to see you", Alma said.

They arrived around noon, and Alma showed them inside. The room was small but very nicely arranged. Sam and Alma liked one another from the first sight.

"It's lunch time, and you all must be famished", Sam said. "Let's go eat and have a nice talk over a hot meal."

On the way out, she said:

"I know very well this town and the campus. I've worked here my first two years after graduation. It's a reputable university and a great place to work. I only moved to Austin because I was offered a higher position and a better pay, otherwise I would have stayed here. I also know well the library where you work, Alma and I must say that is the best one I know."

They had lunch and talked a lot, every one racing to tell what happened lately in their lives. Philip and Mat refrained from recounting the sharp scene they had recently with Nora. It was already late afternoon when they went to see Mya and Nana; they both looked tired since they came from work shortly before. It was Saturday, but they had to work according to the schedule. The four newcomers took seats in the living room, and talking and laughing seemed never to end. Late evening when ready to go, Sam said:

"I wish I had a family like yours, and I'm very happy I've met you."

"Sam you're a wonderful person", Mya said and I hope you'll come again."

"I join Mya and must say that you're now a dear member of our family", Nana added.

They embraced each other, and the four of them left.

"Tomorrow is Sunday and maybe we can stay for the day", Mat suggested.

"Why not? I would be delighted. What do you think Philip?", Sam asked.

"With great pleasure. Let's go to the hotel and the kids will go wherever they must go."

The next day was full of joy and everyone had the good feeling of being so close to each other.

Meantime, Nora felt like a wreck, and as usually, when she was sluggish or needed help she ran to her brother for support. She flew to Midland and told Jack about the hard scene she had with Philip.

"Your mind is confused many times and you have to manage your reasoning that often does not work for you", he said. "I supported you whenever you messed things up, but not this time, sister. I like Philip and I like Mat, they are good, honest, and considerate people, and you hurt them badly. I'm not going to help you hurting them even more than you did. Go home and find a way to make peace with them, if you can, or he will leave you like a nobody, and without any regrets."

"He will not divorce me, because he needs the farm for his work", Nora said.

"Don't count on it. He is recognized as one of the greatest scientists of his generation, and believe me little sister, he can do his work without your farm. As far as I know, Mat is following in his father's footsteps, and he doesn't need your farm either. You'll be left alone, Nora, and have only your worthless friends to whom to speak and with whom to enjoy your parties. You might be very rich with the wealth you have, but let me tell you something sister: you're very poor, because you lost the most valuable people in your life."

Nora returned home, in her big, luxurious mansion, where everything was just emptiness. She needed to do something with her time, trying to forget about her shaking marriage. In that summer she started the project of remodeling the house, thinking that one day she will have a grandchild to raise there. She admitted that she was not a good mother, but when she will have a grandchild, she will prove that her natural instincts will change. Thinking about that future, Nora made already a sketch of her plans. She will find a rich girl for Mat, one that will belong to her high class of wealthy people; they will get married and give her a grandchild. Then she will raise him like her own, according to the high level of her league, and teaching him her own rules of survival. With these thoughts in her mind, Nora felt much better and more convinced that she will accomplish her plans with big success, totally neglecting the perspective of Mat's and Philip's feelings which could be different from hers.

Time went by, Alma entered the second year of college and Mat the third. They kept seeing each other like before, making more solid plans for their future, which will be after they both will finish school and have a career. Mat continued to join his father on the farm and work together in the lab. He acquired over the years a lot of knowledge being far ahead his colleagues who pursued the same career. Alma was already much appreciated for her professional attitude and for her dedication to the job. At one of the work analysis meetings, the Director of Library, by his name Luke Bradley, congratulated her in front of the other employees for performing an excellent job. The personnel in the library were friendly, consulting each other on the job, helping with information and knowledge, but never socialized.

One day at closing time, Alma was about to leave, when the Director approached her outside the building:

"Miss Reid, I see that you don't have a car. May I give you a ride? Where do you live?"

"Thank you kindly, Director, but I live on campus in a dorm, just a few steps from here."

"Then, may I accompany you for those few steps?"

"I'll be very pleased, thank you."

In that short walk, he asked her about school, about her plans for a career, and about her work in the library.

"I noticed that you're very dedicated on your job and I'm sure you'll become a highly qualified librarian and a successful writer. Your family must be very proud of you."

"Yes, they are. My father was a foreman on a farm, died a couple of years ago and my mother, my aunt, and I, we moved here. My mother works in a bakery, not far from the campus, my aunt is a nurse and works at the children hospital. We see each other only on weekends, but we are very close. If you remember, some of these are answers to the questions you asked me two years ago when I applied for the job."

"Yes I remember, but I wanted to know if you and your family are pleased with your position and with your job."

"We are, and I appreciate your concern. Here is my dorm. Thank you for your kindness. Good night, Director."

"Good night Miss Reid, it has been a pleasure."

Alma told Mat about that conversation with the Director and how nice he was to her.

"Maybe he becomes too nice to you. What is his name?"

"Why? Do you want to check on him?"

"Just asking."

"Luke Bradley, and for your information, he is the age of my father, maybe even older, has white hair, and a white goatee beard. This satisfies you?"

"Old men like young women, that's what I know. I love you more than anything in the world and I don't like anyone coming close to you."

"Stop it! I like you better when you talk sense and not being childish!"

He mumbled something in Greek, and kissed her with all the warmth of his soul. She loved him no less and felt the same.

One day, Alma was called to the office of the Director. He started with a straightforward approach :

"My daughter, Erin, is about your age and has Multiple Sclerosis. She finished college and made plans to become a school teacher when the illness struck her. My wife left us and divorced me, without showing any regrets for our daughter. The caregiver we had, is getting married and has to leave. You told me that your aunt works in a hospital, and maybe she might recommend someone skilled and trustworthy who can take care of Erin. She will have her own room, food, and a good salary. Can you help me, Miss Reid?"

"I'm very sorry for your daughter. I certainly can talk to my aunt, and I'm sure she might know a skilled nurse who will be interested to take the job. I'll talk to her tonight, and I'll let you know."

In that evening, Alma told Nana about her boss's request.

"What exactly is Multiple Sclerosis, Nana?"

"It's an unpredictable disease of the central nervous system that disrupts the flow of information within the brain, and between the brain and the spinal cord. It's considered an autoimmune disease in which the body's immune system mistakes part of the body for a foreign substance and attacks its own tissues. The cause is unknown and the disease has no cure. MS can occur at any age, but onset usually occurs around twenty and forty years of age. The symptoms are vision problems, tingling and numbness, weakness, dizziness, pain and spasms, among others. Maybe I'll take the job, Alma. I'm getting tired of the tight schedule, being all day long on my feet, and of riding two buses every day, back and forth. What do you think?"

"I don't know Nana what to say, because I don't know how sick that girl is, and how much care she needs. Nevertheless, you can talk to my boss, and we'll go together to find out about the entire situation. If you decide to take the job, it's only up to you, and if not, there will be no harm done. I don't want you to take a job, which will make you unhappy, only because the sick girl is the daughter of my boss. Come tomorrow if you can, to the library, and we'll see."

Nana took the day off, and showed up in the morning at Alma's desk. They went together to the Director's office and had a long talk.

"Would you like us to go to my house and see my daughter? We can go now, if you're not busy, and I would like Miss Reid to accompany us."

He lived in the suburbs and took them more than an hour to get there. The two-story house was very big, with balconies all around the second floor, and had a flower garden in front, which looked well maintained. The inside was very spacious, with elegant furniture, and very clean. A stair lift for disabled was installed for Erin, to make her easy going up and down.

The Director asked them to step inside and said:

"Erin is upstairs, let's go, and see her."

The room was very big and had lots of light coming from outside. She was sitting in a wheelchair and the caregiver just finished feeding her. Saying that she was beautiful would be too little said. She had auburn, curly hair, almond shaped gray eyes with flecks of gold and brown, and her smile was exquisite. Her father made the introductions and Erin said:

"I'm very pleased to meet you Alma, I've heard

a lot about you and everything the best. Ms. West, my father told me about you and maybe we'll know each other on permanent basis. Please have a seat."

"I'll be happy to know you better, Miss Bradley. Please call me Nana, everybody does. May I call you Erin?"

"Certainly, I like that. Do you know about my illness, and how to treat it, Nana?"

"Yes, Erin, I know a lot about it. I'm a registered nurse and I've seen many cases like yours. What I'd like to do now, is to have a few minutes in private with you, if Director and Alma allow me."

The two of them stepped outside, and went to the other room talking about the event.

"You can call me Luke", he said, "when we're not on the job. May I call you Alma, also when we're not on the job?"

"Of course, I like that", she said.

After about half hour, Nana called them in. She gave Erin a short checkup mostly at her mobility, vision, and nerve reflex. She was sure that Erin didn't have the home treatment she needed all the time, but didn't say anything, except:

"I'll take the job, Director, and I'll be glad to do my best in taking care of Erin."

"Please call me Luke. I'll be happy to have you here, knowing that my daughter is in the best hands. What do you think, Erin?"

"I think Nana would be wonderful for this job, Dad. She seems very skilled, knowing what she's doing, and besides, she is very kind, nice, and considerate. I think we'll have a splendid relationship. When can you start, Nana?"

"Next week. What I would like you to do until then is to follow the exercises I showed you, and not skip one day. Promise?"

"Yes, I promise."

They said goodbye to each other and her father said:

"I'm very happy that Nana decided to take the job. I'll see you tonight, dearest."

Before starting the job, Luke told Nana that she will have her own room, food as much as she liked, and Sunday will be her day off, when he will take care of Erin. The salary he mentioned was impressive.

Mya was very happy for Nana, even if she will miss her seeing every day, but they will have a lot to talk about on Sundays when Nana will be home. Alma told Mat about what happened lately and what a wonderful person Erin was.

"You think that this is a good move for Nana?", he asked.

"I think this is very good for her. She got tired working at the hospital, especially riding two buses every day. It's a good place for her to work there and she likes that kind of job."

"How long can Erin live?"

"With care and right treatment she can live long enough and have a productive life."

Alma went quite often to see Erin, and slowly they became good friends. Sometimes, Mat accompanied her and they liked each other a lot; they were about the same age and had a lot in common to talk about. Alma told her about her life on the farm, about her modest family; her father was a foreman and her mother cooked for the workers. She told her about Mat, how they grew up together and how much they love each other. She told her about Philip and Nora, how different one from another was, and what an unconcerned mother she was for Mat since he was born. Nana became acting mother for Mat and raised him like her own. Philip was a brilliant scientist and Mat is following in his father's footsteps, studying to become a professor and a scientist; they are extremely close to one another. When Alma and Mat will finish school they'll get married, even if Nora might stay in their way, just because Alma didn't come from a rich and famous family.

Erin told Alma about her mother who left her and her father, and her departure was very hard to handle for both of them. She also told her that she was in love with a colleague in college, made plans for their future, but when she was struck by the disease, he ran away, saying that he couldn't share his life with a disabled woman. Erin suffered a lot, and it took her a long time to recover. She finished college and couldn't wait to become a school teacher, but her illness was a much too big impediment to fulfill her dream. Now, she was sitting there in that wheelchair, without any perspective for her future. Alma came up with a suggestion:

"I think it will help you keeping your mind active, and even it will be a satisfaction for you, if you open a website answering questions to children and teenagers about their problems. You're a teacher, and this will be a good place for you to practice the talent you have. What do you say?"

"You know what? I think this is a wonderful idea, Alma. I'm very good with computers and I love to work with children at all ages. I'll make a website, I'll place an ad, and see what happens."

Not long after, questions from children of all ages started pouring out. Erin was so excited that she completely forgot about her illness and she felt like she was awakened from a nightmare. Her attitude changed a lot, she was radiant, laughed and told jokes, and she could make some steps around the room helped by a cane. Tingling and numbness, weakness, dizziness, pain and spasms became less acute, making Nana extremely happy. Now, she had a girl to be a mother to.

Luke called Alma to his office, one day.

"I don't know what you and Nana did to my daughter, but I must say that a miracle happened to her. She changed a lot, found something worth living since you advised her to open that website and work with children. Also, Nana applied her home treatment with massages and baths that proved to be very successful. Most of all, her mind is much clearer and no longer covered with sadness as it was. I tried many times to make her think positively, telling her that she could have a quiet and acceptable life in spite of her illness, but she didn't respond to my advice. What I tried for such a long time without result, you succeeded in a little while, and I don't know how to thank you."

"No need to thank me. I'm glad I could help. You see, Luke, you're an erudite, because you studied and read a lot, acquiring a huge knowledge, but you neglected what was most important: Erin needed a purpose close to her desires and her vocation to fight for and which would have galvanized her mind. She had few choices, but as long as there were some, she could pick one and set a goal to achieve. What to think positively if there is nothing there to think about? When the mind works properly, the body follows, and maybe you forgot about this too. If Erin stays with the purpose she found, she will have a good and productive life."

"How can you be so smart at your age?"

"I learned from bad and good experiences, and in spite of being young, I had a lot of both."

Alma told Mat what happened lately, and how Erin improved her state of mind and her physical condition, by working on her website.

"You're the most resourceful girl I know", he said.

"How many girls do you know?"

"One."

In the meantime, the improvements of the mansion on the farm were finished, with more rooms, bathrooms, and halls. One Saturday morning, Nora came to the lab where Philip and Mat worked on a project.

"Tomorrow is Sunday, we'll have a party with most prominent people coming with families, and I would like you both to attend it."

"I'm busy with a project that can't be delayed and I have to work on my papers which are at school", Philip said.

"What about you?", she asked Mat.

"I'm not a partygoer."

"You can meet people of your age and I'm sure that you must have lot in common to talk about."

"I'm not much of a talker, and apart from seeds, cells, molecules, and genes, I don't know what else to talk about. These subjects won't be of any interest to your guests."

"Maybe you'll meet a nice girl and you could entertain her."

"I'm shy and awkward with girls, and I'm not an entertainer for your guests."

"You two will make me look very bad in front of everyone who will be there."

"Nora, you never look bad when it comes to

your rich and powerful friends. You are always on top of them, and you always enjoy an old companion that certainly must be there for you. We don't need to come to your party, and play happy family", Philip said.

She turned around and left slamming the door. They both had a good laugh.

"What are your plans for this weekend?", Philip asked.

"I have to go to that jeweler in Tilden. Two weeks ago, I ordered an engagement ring for Alma, to be my fiancée. It must be ready, and then I'll drive to see her and we'll get engaged forever. Don't worry about the money; I've already paid for it from my trust fund. How about you?"

"You gave me an idea. I'll go and pick up Sam, we'll join you and the family, and tomorrow we'll celebrate your engagement. Sounds good?"

"Awesome!"

The ring was indeed a superb work of art. It had an emerald stone and a diamond, touching each other. The inscription inside said: *together forever.*

Mat drove directly to Alma's room. She was writing and looked very busy, but jumped with joy when he stepped in.

"Princess Alma would you be my fiancée?"

"I'm your fiancée since I was born and you were one year old. Why now?"

"Now we are mature and I want to seal our love forever."

"Why seal our love? It's not going anywhere. Before I answer to your question I must tell you this: Matheo Doukas, you are the most loved man on this planet, and I'll love you the same until I'll die. Now I can say, yes, Prince Matheo, I'll be delighted to be your mature fiancée."

Mat opened the small box with the ring, and said:

"I adore you and I cherish you for as long I'll be alive."

He put the ring on her finger and kissed her with passion.

"These are our birthstones, yours is diamond and mine is emerald! Mat, I'll never take this ring off my finger."

When she read the inscription, she started crying, and he joined her.

"I'm scared of so much happiness, Mat, what if something bad will happen to us?"

"I cannot answer that nothing bad will happen to us, because anything is possible; I can tell you this: no matter what it will be, I'll adore you until I'll die."

"Me too."

Philip and Sam came late afternoon congratulating them both for their engagement, and admiring Alma's ring.

"It's not only very beautiful, but also powerfully

evocative, since it will always bring images, memories, and feelings to your mind", Sam said.

"You speak like a philosopher, because you are one, but I am a father and couldn't say it better", Philip completed her remark. "I spoke to Mya, she said that she is very tired and wouldn't be able to join us for dinner. Nana is still at work and she will have the day off tomorrow. So, the four of us, will go to dinner with dance and music, and celebrate your engagement."

They all agreed with big enthusiasm and late evening went to the best restaurant in town. They talked a lot, laughed, and danced until after midnight. The next day they went to see Mya and Nana who told them everything what happened to them lately. Both were extremely happy for Alma and Mat, whishing them the best in their lives.

Time went by, bringing new developments with emotional responses, featuring love, tenderness, and distress, of those people who believed in trust, honesty, and looked out for each other.

Alma finished college with bachelor degree in Library Science, and enrolled in Master of Library and Information Studies (MLIS) program which could be achieved in one-two years, to become a university librarian. Her major degree was in English and English Literature to become a writer. She was promoted to Library Associate position, with permanent job, and she moved from her campus room to an one bedroom apartment not far from the library. In the same time, she wrote and published a book inspired by her life on the farm, which was well received in the literary community.

Mat entered the second year of graduate school studying for his doctorate degree (PhD) in Molecular Biology and Genetics. Usually it takes four to six years to finish the program, but because he had lot of experience in laboratory and research, and also his father was his advisor for his thesis, he intended to get his degree in two years. Unlike the other students working for doctoral degree, Mat had published over the years many research papers, which were well received by the scientific community. His persevering activity in the field of research has contributed to reducing the time for obtaining his doctoral degree. He was considered one of the few students belonging to the academic elite in the university.

Mya's life became totally different when the wife of his boss died from diabetes. She became master baker and a young girl was hired as kitchen help. Not long after, she started dating her boss, who was ten years older than she was but they liked each other and they found to have lot in common. He had a house not far from the bakery and asked Mya to move with him. She didn't have second thoughts, told Alma and Nana who were surprised but accepted the situation just the way it was. Mya gave up her apartment, since Nana was in town only for the Sundays and could stay with Alma for the day.

Nana kept taking good care of Erin and both became fond of each other. The home treatment she applied everyday, combined with the prescription medication with regular visits to the doctor, proved to work well. Regularly, when weather was favorable, Nana drove Erin to the park and there they had short walks with pauses, for about one hour. Almost every Sunday, Nana went to see Alma and Mat, but many times she chose not to go and instead, to stay home with Erin. Somehow, she understood that she had no other place in life, even if she dearly loved her adoptive family.

Erin's life style changed a lot since she opened that website to work with children. Even though her illness had no cure, at least it was showing signs of not worsening. Her mind was active and she was in good spirit most of the time, making her father and Nana very happy. She helped hundreds of children with family or illness problems, to cope with difficult situations and to find an appropriate way of dealing with their sufferings. Alma used to come visit her from time to time and they had long talks about everything that happened to them lately. They became good friends over the passing years, caring for each other and knowing that if in need, each one of them could help the other one, if only by sharing their thoughts and feelings.

Philip continued to work as a professor and

at the same time continued his research in the laboratory. The ten-acre area for the experiments was covered with hybrid plants that he had experimented through molecular research on photosynthetic organisms and had been unknown until then. A delegation of scientists and professors were invited to the farm to observe his work and make the necessary comments on the results of his experiments. They filmed and photographed, and some of them measured the consistency of plants in phenolic acids that are beneficial to health and are linked to antioxidant activity. An award ceremony followed in honor of Philip, which was attended by scientific, political and social prominent personalities. His discoveries proved the increase almost doubled in food production as well as in raising the quality of crops on farms. For his outstanding merits, Philip was awarded with one of the highest distinctions in his field. In his speech of acceptance the award, he emphasized the contribution to his research of his assistants among which was his son, Matheo Doukas who recently obtained the doctoral degree in Microbiology and Genetics. Alma, Sam, and Mat were there and felt like starting crying. Huge applauses followed, everyone approaching Philip and congratulating him. It was an evening to remember and never to be forgotten.

Nora found out about the award ceremony and revolted angrily at Philip:

"Why wasn't I invited? I heard that all scientists and professors came with their wives!"

"In case you forgot, we are separated for more than twenty years, and you're no longer my wife."

"Legally I'm still your wife!"

"Not anymore. I've introduced the divorce papers, and you'll get them this week to be signed. You'll not be called anymore 'Mrs. Doukas', but just 'Mrs. Wilson', because I specified this clause in the divorce petition."

"How dare you? I'll make it very hard for you, so that you'll end up with nothing. You'll lose the farm, did you think about that?"

"You can keep the farm, and everything else, because I don't need anything from you, except that I don't want to see you or hear about you for as long as I live."

"We'll see. Are you having an affair?"

"No, I don't have an affair, and I don't need one to get rid of you." (I have the love of my life, he said to himself).

Nora turned around slamming the door. She was ravaged by anger and all her thoughts and feelings circled in her mind to hatch a plot.

Philip and Mat went to the farm and took only the equipment which was paid by them, and only their belongings.

The divorce papers were served to Nora by Philip's attorney, but she refused to sign them. His attorney filed a request to enter a default divorce, the court set a hearing date when only Philip appeared with his attorney and the judge issued a ruling based entirely on what was stated in the divorce petition. Since there were no financial and property issues, the court granted the divorce orders and judgment.

Nora was enraged like never before. She expected Philip to claim his part of the farm, and when she was notified by his attorney that he didn't request any property or equivalent of assets, her anger went through the roof.

In the coming weekend, Philip and Sam got married in a small ceremony attended only by their family. Mat couldn't be happier.

When Nora heard about Philip's marriage, her rage went ballistic; she started smashing and throwing things around the house, yelling in the same time like in hell:

"How could I've been so stupid in believing that he was incapable of dealing with women?! I thought all the time that he only was interested in keeping his nose into his plants and nothing else! Certainly, he must have had an affair with that woman for a long time and was clever enough to hide it so carefully that I never could find out about! If I knew, I would have destroyed him like a mouse! He made a mockery out of me all this time! I'll become the laughing stock of all my friends!"

And so on and on, she kept yelling and smashing everything around her. After a couple of days she packed her things and flew to Midland. There, she told her brother how Philip had made fun of her, certainly for a long time.

"You did it to yourself, Nora. I advised you many times to find a way of being nice and civilized to him, but you never listened. You always want to be in control and above the others, not caring a bit of what other people think or feel. With your antagonistic attitude, you hurt people's feelings, you do damage to their confidence, and you alienate them. You always want to be recognized as being somebody who has big power because you have big money. Life is not what you want it to be. Everyone has choices, opinions, beliefs, and you should respect them if you want to be respected. Money means nothing compared to being loved, cherished, respected, and wanted. You lost the most honest and considerate people you had around because of your arrogance, your selfishness and your belief that you were superior to them. I cannot give you any advice to make you feel better, because I don't know anymore what to tell you. Find your way to get over your distress, because you're alone."

Nora burst out crying, packed again her things, and flew back to Austin.

In the meantime, Alma and Mat got married, having the love and care of their family around. As wife and husband, the bond between them became stronger than it could be. Mat was appointed associate professor working at the same university as his father, with whom he continued to do scientific research as before. Alma was very appreciated in her job as library assistant, and in the same time she wrote and published a second book, with short stories this time. One day, Mat came home and said:

"Summer vacation starts Monday, let's go somewhere….."

"I'm pregnant and…."

He interrupted her, kissing and kissing her over and over. Finally, he managed to articulate a few words:

"I'll be the best father a child could have. I promise. I really promise, my dearest of all. I'll share with you the care for him day and night and you'll never have to worry about anything, ever. I promise….."

This time she interrupted his stammering speech, kissing him over and over again.

They told Philip and Sam who were overjoyed and showed big concern.

"You have to keep doctor's appointments all the time, have lot of rest and good nutrition", Philip said, and Sam added:

"We both are here for you, anytime and with everything you need, just ask."

"Thank you both, I know what to do and I'm happy to have you close to me. Just tell Mat not to suffocate me with his worries and not to be scared like a little child. I'll be fine, I promise."

Mat was like a mother hen around her, worried and happy in the same time. When talking about the name of the child, Mat said:

"If it's a boy, I would like to name him *Philip* after my father, but again, there will be two célèbre scientists with same name, and this will be confusing. If it's a girl I would like to name her *Thea* after my paternal grandmother. What do you think?"

"I think it's too early for choosing the name", Philip said.

"I think that Alma has the right to say a word, too", Sam said, "tell us Alma what would be your choice."

"Thank you Sam for giving me the right to speak, since nobody else seems to notice that I'm alive. If it's going to be a boy, I'll choose the name *Andrew* after my paternal grandfather, and if it's a girl I would like to name her *Ella* after my maternal grandmother."

"Now we all know, and since the mother of the child is Alma, she has priority in choosing the name for her child", Philip said.

One day, a young woman showed at Mat's office. She was medium high, red hair, big, round blue eyes, had freckles, and wore glasses.

"Good morning, Professor Doukas, I am Rose Wright, and I would appreciate a few minutes of your time to talk with you about a matter which concerns us both."

"Good morning Ms. Wright, but I don't see what matter might concern us both, since I don't know you, or who you are. Do we have a common acquaintance, maybe?"

"Yes, we do. Your mother and my mother. Would this be enough for a common acquaintance?"

"Oh, really! Yes, this would be enough. What seems to be the problem?"

"It's a long story, and it requires a little bit more time for me to tell you about. If you don't mind I would rather like us to go some place where we can talk."

"Meet me in an hour at the park entrance."

They made a short walk in the park and sat on a side bench that was not in the public eye.

"Start talking, Ms. Wright."

"You can call me Rose. May I call you Mat, since we're about the same age?"

"Call me what you want, just start talking."

"My mother is Claire Wright, and maybe you heard about her."

"The cosmetics mogul? Everybody heard about her."

"Yes, and she is a good friend of your mother, for quite a long time."

"This doesn't surprise me; they're both very rich, and certainly they both believe in the boundless power of money which can buy anything and anyone."

"Correct. When I was a little child, my mother was a modest vendor in a small cosmetics boutique, and my father was an accountant. At my very young age, my father left us for another woman, and my mother raised me alone, struggling with a small salary and barely keeping up with the cost of living. One day, she made an application for financial aid to open her own business. Slowly, her money grew until she became rich, and in time, she became the cosmetics mogul of today. She was always busy and I grew the way I could, learning in a good boarding school, coming home only for vacation, and seeing my mother whenever she found time for me. We were not very close, but we understood well each other, enough to tolerate each other's character and behavior. I went to college and became a high school teacher; I've met a young man, Jim by his name, and we fell in love. He also was a teacher and we planned to get married as soon as we'll have enough to stand on our own feet, without help from our families. My mother found out and got crazy. She reminded me how much we struggled to survive because her earning was barely enough to pay for food and rent. She mentioned with a high pitch in her voice that she'll never allow me to marry a poor man and count the money from one day to the next. She mentioned many insults and offensive descriptions of the man

I loved, against the fact that I tried to explain the reality to her from my point of view. Finally, I gave up arguing, and together with Jim, we decided to wait and see what to do next. I must tell you, Mat, that Jim is the love of my life, and he means everything to me. We might even consider to elope, and hide somewhere in a place to live in peace and far away from my mother's long arm. I'm pregnant, and this is one more reason to look for a solution to solve our problem, because if my mother finds out, she will destroy Jim first. Now, you come into the scene. Nora knows that you and Alma are in love and intend one day to get married. The same as my mother, she doesn't want you to marry a girl from the low class of workers on the farm. You two grew up together and both are each other's love of life. Don't ask how I found out. My mother and your mother, they both planned for us to meet and start a love affair. Nora wants badly to have a grandchild, to raise him as her own and make of him the heir of her wealth. If Alma had a child, she planned to take it away from her, even kidnapping it and hide it in some place where no one could find it. She plans to talk to Alma and offer her a huge amount of money to let you go free, and if she refuses, Nora will take all the measures in her power to destroy her, and not only her, but your father also. Believe me, she can do it, and she'll not have second thoughts to achieve her diabolic plan. As you can see, this is a well-crafted plan that could serve both parties, my mother's and Nora's.

"I'm stunned and horrified, Rose. What are we going to do? I'm completely numb."

"I'll tell you what you can do. Take your beloved Alma and run as far as possible. Hide for the time being in a place where even Nora's long arm will not be able to reach you. I suggest overseas. Don't tell the others here where you're going unless you trust them with your life. I have some very reliable friends in France, and they can help you until you'll find a job to support yourselves. I'll give you their address. Don't waste your time, Mat, because you and Alma are in serious danger."

"What are you going to do, Rose?"

"Don't worry about me. I've learned from my mother how to fight people who mean harm to me, and she became one of them. I'll be her worst nightmare until she will give up and let me and Jim alone. We'll get married and we'll raise our child to be a decent, honest, and considerate human being to cherish the inner values and not the money of the rich and famous people."

"I hope you're right, Rose. You are very courageous and very honest. I sincerely appreciate everything you told me, even if I'm horrified."

"I'll tell you something else that could give you more time until you'll find the most suitable solution. This coming Saturday, Nora will give a party for her friends; my mother and I, we are invited. She intends to call you and ask you to attend her party, because she says, this will give you the chance to meet prominent people who might become useful to your career. The real reason is to lure you into meeting me and start courting me. I'm supposed to be the bait to get rid of both, Alma and Jim; don't refuse her, but accept the invitation. I promise, we will have fun at their expense thinking that they believe in the success of their plot."

"I'll come. I wish you and Jim the best in your life and I hope everything will work for you the way you want. Thank you for everything you told me. I'll see you Saturday. Goodbye, Rose."

She took out of her pocket a small recorder and gave it to him.

"I have something for you. I've recorded our entire conversation, so that you have everything on tape. Ask especially Alma and Philip to listen to it and take it very seriously. Bye Mat, we'll see each other this Saturday."

Mat went back to his office, feeling like a shadow and not anymore being alert at what was going around him. He sat on his chair, keeping his head in his hands, and trying to think. He called Philip:

"Take Sam and both come to my home this evening."

"We have tickets to the theater."

"Just come!"

Late evening they both came and Philip asked:

"What was so important that couldn't wait?"

"Everyone, take a seat and listen to this", Mat said.

He turned on the recorder, and slowly everyone's attention grew until signs of being shocked appeared on their faces. Alma became pale, gasping for air, and fainted before the recorder stopped.

The paramedics were called; they revived her and rushed her to the hospital. The doctor checked her thoroughly, and said:

"She will be fine, and her pregnancy goes well, but it seems that she was under lot of stress lately, and this affects her mind. I gave her a medication to reduce the stress, and I'll keep her here overnight for observation. There is no need for you to stay, you can go home and come in the morning."

"I'll stay with her", Mat said "and you two go home and can sleep in our bedroom. We'll see you in the morning."

He sat next to Alma keeping her hand all night long. In the morning the doctor said that Alma was all right, only she had to avoid stress. They went home where Sam cooked already breakfast but no one was hungry. They all were concerned about the difficult situation told by Rose, and which apparently had no solution.

"What are we going to do?", Mat asked.

"I was thinking all night and after analyzing

several possibilities from among a series of choices, I would say that overseas is the only one which could keep you safe", Philip said. "I have a friend from England who came here to study and we graduated in the same time. His name is Oscar Davies. He went back and became Dean of the University of Bristol, which is located in the South West of United Kingdom and is about one hundred miles far from London. Bristol is one of the top ten universities out there and among others, it has a research school in Biological Sciences that spans the full range of biological disciplines, from genomics and cell biology, through diverse aspects of whole organism biology and evolution, to population biology and ecosystem services. I'll give a call to Oscar and I'll tell him that my son, who recently obtained his doctoral degree, would very much like to have British experience in one of England's prestigious school, like Bristol. I'll ask him to find a position for my son, even if not full professor, but maybe assistant. If he can, I'm sure he will help me. What do you say?"

"Sounds awesome, Dad, but we'll be far away from our family for a long time."

"Would you rather hide in a village, or in a small town, or working undercover on a farm?"

"I join your father, Mat, and think that this would be the best solution for you both. I know that Bristol also has a huge library where Alma can work and I'm sure that her experience will be appreciated."

"I think you're both right and you two are marvelous people who care about us", Alma said.

"One more thing, and maybe this is the most important: your baby will be born there and will become British citizen. Nobody in the whole world would be able to touch him, and I must mention, that the laws there are very strong and powerful when it comes to their citizens. Even if you surface up, Nora cannot do a damn thing."

"This is breathtaking, Dad! I never thought about that!"

"I'll call Oscar now, since it's the right time; United Kingdom is six hours ahead of Austin."

Alma and Mat went to Erin's house; Luke happened to be home, and Nana joined them when Alma said that something important is for them to know. Mat turned on the recorder, and everyone became extremely shocked.

"What are you going to do?", Erin asked.

"We plan to go to France for a while, settle there, and find a job. France is a big country, and it will be hard, if not impossible for Nora to find us", Mat said. "My father will be in touch with you and let you know about our whereabouts. We have to leave now, and I must say that you'll always be in our hearts."

Mat and Alma left before starting crying. They

went to Mya's house and told her the same story. She exploded in rage:

"I knew that Nora was a bad woman but never thought she'll be like that!"

"We'll be fine, Mom", Alma said "and she'll never find us. We'll be gone for a while and we'll see each other maybe sooner than you think."

They left, leaving Mya in tears, and knowing that it's going to be a long time until they might see her again, perhaps never.

In the coming days, Nora called Mat:

"I'm having a party this coming Saturday, and I would like very much you to come. There will be prominent people who are eager to meet you, and you can use some high connection for your career. You're now on summer vacation and I was thinking that you can attend my party. Would you come?"

"I'm really very busy, but I'll come. Thanks for the invitation."

In the coming Saturday, Mat went to Nora's party. She opened the door and exclaimed:

"Mat! It's so good to see you! Come in!"

She took him by the hand but he avoided her contact.

There were probably around fifteen people inside, in small groups, chatting and laughing; a huge buffet was on display along the opposite wall. Rose and her mother saw Mat coming in and approached him; Nora made the introduction:

"Claire, Rose, this is my son Mat, and this is my very good friend Claire Wright and her daughter, Rose."

"You're indeed very handsome, Mat, just like your mother said. May I call you Mat?"

"I'm pleased to meet you Mrs. Wright, and you may call me 'Doctor or Professor Doukas', since we're not a same generation, but you Rose can call me Mat, since we're about the same age."

"I'm very pleased to meet you Mat", Rose said and smiled.

The music invited the guests on the floor for a smooth dance; Mat mumbled some excuses before Nora and Claire, and asked Rose to dance with him.

"Is he always so grumpy?", Claire asked.

"He cares a lot about his titles and his name and displays them whenever he has the opportunity; notice that he is very kind to your daughter. Maybe we'll go somewhere from the first step without much intervention. Come, let them dance and talk and we'll mingle with the crowd."

"You're a very good dancer, Mat. Tell me what you decided. Try smiling when you talk and remember, you're supposed to court me."

"We chose England, and we'll settle there, even if we'll tell the family for time being, that we're going to France. I don't know much what to say, until we'll go there, and find a job. For now though, we'll tell everyone that for the summer vacation, we're going to Florida wilderness, where there is no phone and they can't reach us. My father will stay in touch with you and you'll know about our whereabouts. What about you, Rose?"

"After you leave the scene and can't be found, I'll tell my mother I'm pregnant and then she won't have anything to look for and will accept Jim; I know her very well. She is very ambitious but she is not a bad person. When she'll have a grandchild, she will be thrilled and will adore it. In short time she will even start liking Jim and find out what a good man he is. Don't worry about me; when my child will be born I'll set the conditions in my relationship with my mother, and be sure that she will comply with all of them. Now, you should mingle with those people, exchange a few words, and then go."

"I wish I could hug you, Rose, but I only can say that I shall always remember you as a good and dear friend. I wish you and Jim all the best and maybe, one day we'll meet each other again. Good bye my dear friend."

"Good bye dear Mat, I'll never forget you either; take care of you and Alma."

Mat mingled with the crowd, exchanged a few words with some of the people, and told Nora that he had to leave. Claire was next to her.

"Why so soon? I saw that you and Rose talked a lot", Nora said.

"I have some papers to finish. Yes, we talked

a lot and Rose is a very intelligent and agreeable person. We found many subjects to discuss and it was a very pleasant evening for us both."

"Are you going to see each other again?", Claire asked.

"Of course. I must go now. It was a pleasure meeting you, Mrs. Wright. Good night, Ladies."

Mat went home and told everyone how successful was the party.

"For the time being we don't have to worry about Nora's plan; she was very pleased with my good behavior."

"You start packing and next week you both go; Dean Davies is waiting for you", Philip said.

"We don't have passports Dad", Mat said.

"Go to this address, to this office, and ask for the name of this officer; he is waiting for you and he'll give you passports. I have connections at the highest places that I never used, but this time I'm using them."

"Why don't you use your connections to stop Nora's diabolic plans?"

"Without proof nobody can do anything about."

In the coming week, Mat and Alma were ready to bid farewell to Philip and Sam.

"Call us as soon as you get off the plane", Philip said. "It will take you about twelve hours to get to London and I'll sit there in that chair doing nothing but waiting for your call."

"I promise Dad", Mat said. "Not only that, but

we can see each other on laptop, every time, day or night. Please, you two, take care of one another, and let us know about every move you make. To say that we're going to miss you, is very little and I don't have the right words to say how I feel."

"You both gave us love, and care, and compassion at every step in our lives", Alma said. "If I would know that we'll never see each other again, I wouldn't leave, and rather I would fight Nora all the way. Nevertheless, I hope that we'll see each other if not soon, at least after few months, when you'll make time to come visit us."

"We'll come see you as soon as things here will cool off and we'll be sure that there is no danger anymore", Sam said. "I promise and I must say that I can't wait until then. I join Philip in asking to call as soon as you get off the plane. Now give us a big hug and go, or I'll start sobbing."

They hugged with warmth and love and tears, and left.

After about twelve hours, they arrived in London, took the train to Bristol, and went to a hotel nearby the station. In a couple of days, they found a small apartment close to the university, and Mat went to see Dean Davies. His credentials were excellent, since he published in the past years several papers, which were acclaimed in the scientific community. Dean Davies assigned him to the position of Associate Professor, starting in fall. For the time being, Alma didn't need to have a job, and she will stay home taking care of her pregnancy and concentrating on writing her new book. Everything went well for them, even better than expected. When Philip and Sam learned about the wonderful news, they were thrilled and felt relieved from the stress of the past few weeks.

Philip called Rose and told her everything about what happened lately.

"I'm extremely pleased, Doctor Doukas", she said "and I'm relieved that everything came out so well for them. Now, I can start setting my goal that hopefully will work for me and Jim, and then build on top of that foundation the view from my perspective."

"Please Rose, let me know how everything for you and Jim came out. I wish you the best from the bottom of my heart. And please, call me Philip; since you are a good friend of Mat and Alma, I'll be most pleased to be your friend also."

"Thank you for being so kind, Philip. I'll call you as soon as things around me will go the way I want."

Not long after, Nora called Philip and started yelling from the first word:

"Where is Mat?! I'm trying to reach him and he's not answering the phone! Where is he?!"

Philip put the phone on speaker so that Sam could hear everything.

"He is on vacation in Florida wilderness where phone is not working and the closest town is miles away."

"Is Alma with him?"

"Of course, Alma is with him. Where else could she be but with him."

"Oh, darn it! When is he coming back?"

"In September when the school year begins; why are you suddenly so interested in Mat's whereabouts? You never cared where he was or what he was doing. Why suddenly you became so anxious to know about him?"

"That's something that is not concerning you! Let me know when he'll be back!"

She hung up in a rage. Philip and Sam had a big laugh.

After Alma and Mat settled in their new location in Bristol, they communicated daily with the family, seeing each other on the small screen and recounting all the details of their lives. One day, Rose called Philip and told him the good news: after a long conversation with her mother, Claire accepted her relationship with Jim, and consented to their marriage, especially when Rose told her she was expecting a baby. At the thought of becoming a grandmother, Claire became extremely happy and had no objections to her marriage to Jim. Not only that, but Claire completely broke off relations with Nora, when she realized what a dominant and aggressive character her so-called friend had. Philip and Sam were delighted with the good news that Rose communicated to them and in turn told her how well Alma and Mat started their new life.

At the end of October, Alma gave birth to fraternal twins, a boy and a girl. They named them Andrew and Ella, as they had previously decided with the family. Their happiness and that of their family could not be described in simple words.

Alma no longer needed to work and devoted almost all her time to raising the newborns. She also spent part of her time writing books in which she put all her good intentions to please the readers and which from the beginning of the publications received recognition in the literary community. At the same time, Mat was busy with his job at the university and preoccupied with the thought and the desire to be more with Alma and the twins. When he was at home he did not detach himself from them and he wanted to be as useful as possible in raising and caring for them near Alma.

During the Christmas holidays, Philip and Sam flew to Bristol with the intention of staying for two weeks, during which time to meet their grandchildren and enjoy being together. Mya and Nana accompanied them but only for a few days, because their obligations for their work did not allow them to stay longer. The reunion of the whole family was filled with overwhelming joy.

The stormy wind that shook their lives was soothed by the union, care, and love they had for one another. The rays of the sun, accompanied by a gentle breeze, protected them on the path of a bright life, without dangers and without worries.

About the same time Nora paid a visit to Claire with the intention of having a long conversation with her.

"I tried to find Mat everywhere, and found out that he is on vacation in Florida wilderness, where there is no phone and he can't be reached. As soon as he comes back probably in fall, I'll convince him smoothly or harshly to marry Rose. We'll have a big party and we'll bring them together without any doubt."

Claire had a big laugh:

"More harshly than smoothly, fits your style, Nora. Wake up from your fantasies and step into the real world. First, Mat and Alma are married and they moved overseas for good. Second, Rose and Jim are married, and they're expecting a child. We are all happy, and I'm sure that they'll have a good life, shaped by their needs, their love, and their respect for each other. I almost fell for your crooked plan to force Mat and Rose in a totally inappropriate marriage, when I realized that they don't have any feelings for each other, and that money was far from becoming a lure to bring them happiness."

Nora was stunned and at the same time angry.

"I don't believe you saying that Mat and Alma are married and they moved for good overseas. I expected you, Claire, to support my plan to bring Mat and Rose closer and convince them to get married. They would have become the wealthiest couple in the country, by uniting your wealth with mine. We could have grandchildren to raise together, you and me to become envied heirs for their wealth, respected and feared in the elite society of tycoons. You ruined everything I worked for to achieve. Who told you about Mat and Alma getting married?"

"Rose told me; they are very good friends. Regarding your plan, I must say that it was very bad thinking and I'm happy that it fell."

Nora left like a storm trembling from anger and humiliation. She returned to the farm, the only place where she could take refuge without feeling the world's antagonism against her. Slowly, with hesitant steps, she passed from one room to another in which the furniture and the walls had remained the only silent witnesses of a past that had disappeared taking with it all her hopes for fulfilling a happy life. Everything around her was without any resonance of life and only gave her the feeling of an overwhelming silence like that of a cemetery. Years ago there was a time in her life when she could have everything a woman could want in the world, if she had followed the effort to base her desires, hopes and will on the foundation of harmony and human values. The path that she chose and followed, however, was the one that offered her all the satisfactions she sought and were based only on her dominant character; she scared and threatened everyone who didn't comply with her wishes; she neglected her child, thinking that he stole the love of her husband for her; actually, she didn't even know what love was; her moral values were fragile and almost inexistent; the desire to control everyone around her, selfishness, arrogance, disregard for all those who did not correspond to the social class of the rich, and especially the belief that her wealth had unlimited purchasing power of anything and of everyone, formed and strengthened the foundation of her personal existence, which after countless failures collapsed like a castle built of playing cards.

The gusty wind which she forced in the path of all around her, turned against her, and destroyed all that she hoped and desired to accomplish by domination and by imposing her will to lead the lives of those who had been near her; it shattered everything that was touched by the attributes of a destructive character that despised any human value, leaving just a vacuum behind. Her family left her, the friends she liked became detached from her, the path of her life had no prospective, and she was left alone in an unfriendly world, in which the chords of her feelings were stifled as if her soul trod on dust and ashes.